ABOUT THIS BOOK

From the snowy Adirondack Mountains of upstate New York to the magical Glastonbury, England, to small-town America…from dogs and cats to flowers and ghosts…there's something here to warm the cockles of every romance reader's heart.

Praise for "The Best Catch"

"What makes 'The Best Catch' work are the details. Do you name fish? Are pets an investment? Lots of fun here and worth your time."

Romantic Times
Reviewers Choice Award winner
Kristine Grayson

CONTENTS

IN A GARDEN OF LOVE

TEN SWEET STORIES OF BLOSSOMING ROMANCE

DAYLE A. DERMATIS

THEN & NOW

Then

Kim hunched over the pillow in her lap, her tears dripping on the knockoff Laura Ashley pink-and-green flowered pillowcase. She was as high on the twin bed as she could go, her back pressed against the corner of the room where two dark-paneled walls met. Wind rocked the trailer, spitting sleet against the window, creeping its way through unseen cracks so that even though she wore sweatpants, a sweater, and thick socks, and huddled under her ratty pink chenille bedspread, she was cold.

Another North Country winter.

She'd thought she would be getting away from it.

She'd thought she'd be happy, make a new life with Kevin.

Simple Minds' "Don't You Forget About Me" came through her boom box speakers, bringing with it a fresh wave of hot tears. Why she was listening to the mix tape, she didn't know. It was stupid.

She was stupid.

On the wall next to her, hung on a nail, was her calendar.

Today's date, January 30, was encircled with a heart drawn with her favorite purple glitter pen.

Today was the day Kevin shipped to Tinker AFB in Oklahoma, his second assignment after being here at Plattsburgh AFB, New York. She thought she'd be going with him.

Without thinking, she stuck her hand in her sweatpants pocket, curving her fingers around the tiny, hand carved, wooden sleeping dog. Kevin had made it for her when they'd first started dating. It looked just like her beagle, Bagel, right down to the way Bagel would drape his own tail over his nose when he slept.

It had become a habit to rub her thumb on the gleaming-smooth wood when she was stressed.

The artistry, and the sweetness of the gift, set him apart from the stupid boys she'd gone to school with since she was a kid. Plus Kevin had ambition, and he was saving up for a motorcycle, and…

And now he was gone.

She pulled her hand out of her pocket.

The knock on her bedroom door startled her. "What?"

The door opened halfway, and her mother leaned in. Her hair was piled high like Joan Collins in *Dynasty*, which made Kim wince every time she saw it. Her mother was so *old*.

"Dinner time, hon."

Kim could smell the cooked beef and onions and spices, and remembered it was taco night. Usually she helped grate the Velveeta and shred the head of lettuce, but she wasn't speaking to *anybody* in her family right now. She sniffled. "I'm not hungry."

"Hon, you have to eat. You have to stay healthy for…"

Her mom couldn't bring herself to say the words. God, it was humiliating. Kim threw down the pillow. *"Fine."* She'd hoped it would be like the Madonna video for "Papa Don't Preach," with her parents being upset but finally coming around and being on her side. Instead they wouldn't even talk to her about the pregnancy—they'd simply told her, a few days later, that if she wanted to keep the baby, she was going to live with Aunt Julie in Florida until after the baby was born.

Of course, Kim had thought Kevin would propose, take her away to Oklahoma, where they could be a family.

They'd talked about the future, lots. She was sixteen, and smart, so she was going to graduate from high school before her eighteenth birthday. He was so different from the boys she knew in school. He'd enlisted in the Air Force at seventeen, been stationed here, far from his home in California. That in itself had seemed so brave to Kim, who hadn't been farther than Albany or Burlington, Vermont (except for that time her parents took her to Park Safari in Canada when she was a kid).

Then she'd found out she was pregnant, and she told Kevin, and he said he'd figure out what to do next so they'd be together…and then he was *gone*.

She didn't have a phone in her room, even though all her friends did, so it was hard to find a way to call him. She'd ditched school one day and walked to a Stewart's and called him from the pay phone, but he hadn't been in the dorm. (When she got home, she'd been in a world of trouble.)

And today he'd shipped out and left her behind. Left her and the baby growing in her belly.

She loved him, and she didn't understand.

The mix tape switched to "Broken Wings," and she smacked the boom box off and followed her mother out the door.

She didn't want to eat, but she didn't want to hurt the baby, either.

~

Now

Kim cradled the plain ceramic mug between her hands, breathing in the sweet, almost nutty scent of the green tea. Outside, the Portland rain turned Belmont Street into a glittering visage. She was glad the rain had held off until they'd gotten to the Tao of Tea, but she wasn't watching the rain.

She was gazing at her beautiful baby girl sitting across from her, soon to be a bride.

Okay, she was a bit tipsy from the champagne she'd been given at the bridal store while Amber tried on dresses. Didn't matter. She was just happy, and proud.

Her daughter, whipcord slim from a lifetime of cycling and hiking, sipped her chai. Her wavy blond hair was caught up in a ponytail. People sometimes mistook them for sisters, which Kim thought was ridiculous, even though they were only seventeen years apart. She was forty-seven, had the beginnings of crows' feet around her eyes and a few strands of silver mixed with her darker blond hair.

It was mid-afternoon, a relatively quiet time for the restaurant. Patrons chatted at scattered, mismatched wooden tables, sitting on mismatched chairs and stools. Even the teacups and pots and plates were varied, although most had an Asian motif.

Pots of bamboo were tucked into corners, and the dark walls were covered with wooden shelves bearing more teapots or decorated with Chinese scrolls. The owners had turned a modern space into a tranquil tea garden.

"Mom," Amber said. Her teacup chinked as she set it in its saucer. "I have something to tell you."

Kim smiled and thanked the waitress who handed them their orders: mango mochi ice cream balls for her and moon cake for Amber, then said, "As long as you're not going to tell me you've already eloped, I'm all ears."

Amber rolled her eyes, but it was an affectionate gesture

accompanied by a dimpled smile. "After all we went through today? No, the wedding's still on, and it's the real one."

"Thank God," Kim said. She loved Amber's fiancé, Jeff; they'd been together for six years, and he was clearly devoted to her (and vice versa). "Go on, then."

The ice cream balls, wrapped in rice flour shells, were arranged on a long, thin plate decorated with blue pagodas. She stabbed a spoon into one of them.

"I've found my father," Amber said.

Kim paused in the act of stabbing. It no longer seemed important.

Emotions roll through her, folding one over the other like meringue. It had been almost thirty years. She'd sent a couple letters to his parents' house in Minnesota while their baby—Amber, as soon as she'd known it was a girl—grew in her belly. But he'd never called, never written.

She didn't hate him anymore, not like she had when she'd been exiled to Florida, or when she'd sworn and screamed through childbirth, or when she'd been an exhausted teenaged mom who felt utterly unloved and abandoned.

Eventually, she'd made peace with his leaving. He'd been a kid himself...she couldn't blame him for panicking at the idea of being saddled with a wife and kid. And she hadn't been mature enough for those roles either, although she'd managed to figure out the being-a-mother thing.

Yet her heart still twanged, and her mind raced. How was he? Was he bald, fat, in prison? Handsome, rich, confident? *Who* was he, this Kevin three decades later?

Years ago, she'd given Amber her blessing to track him down if Amber wanted to. She'd given Amber every bit of information she had about Kevin—as if Kevin Martin would be easy to find. Kevin, the statistically twenty-third most popular first name in the United States. Martin, the seventeenth most popular last name.

(Coulda been worse, as Kevin had always said. Coulda been Kevin Smith.)

She'd married a great guy when Amber was three, who adored the toddler as much as he adored Kim. She'd loved him right up to the day of his fatal car accident four years ago. She'd never tried to find Kevin, although she occasionally wondered how he was, and hoped he was happy.

Amber seemed fascinated by her moon cake and her fork, not looking at her.

"I didn't realize you'd been looking for him," Kim said. "I'm still okay with it, by the way. Don't worry."

Relief flooded Amber's brown eyes. She'd gotten those eyes from Kevin, along with her wide mouth. Otherwise, she had Kim's features, right down to their near-identical turned-up noses.

"I started thinking about him when Jeff proposed," she admitted. "I'm so excited to have you walk me down the aisle —I don't need anyone else—but I just…" She made a helpless shrug, her watery-blue-and-green infinity scarf rising and falling around her neck. "I'm starting a new phase of life, and I wondered about who I am, and who he was. That sort of thing."

"How did you find him?"

Amber laughed. "You would not *believe* how many Kevin Martins there are on Facebook! It took forever, but I just kept going through them, tossing out the ones that were too young, too old, wrong ethnicity. I narrowed it down to a few —even with the photo you gave me, it was hard to tell—and then I messaged them."

Kim remembered the photo with a tiny pang, deep in her stomach. Kevin's official Airman photo. He'd looked so proud. So handsome. (So young. They'd both been so young.) He'd come from an abusive home and parents who'd repeatedly told him he wouldn't amount to anything.

Getting through Basic Training had been a huge success for him.

"How is he?" Kim asked. The real question.

"He's good. He was actually really happy to hear from me. I wasn't sure he would be. We've emailed, and talked on the phone once. He lives in Tacoma."

That jolted her. "Wow," Kim said. "He's close."

Since that bitterly cold January day, almost thirty years ago, she'd felt as though he was as far away as any human could be. Before Facebook—before the Internet, really, especially for a poor girl in a podunk town in upstate New York—before cell phones, before any easy way to find someone unless you had money to hire a PI.

He might as well had been on the moon.

Not a two-and-a-half-hour drive away. Weirdly, that was the thing that rattled her the most right now. She picked up her tea, took a swallow of the hot, fragrant liquid to calm herself.

"He's divorced," Amber went on, flaking the crust off her cake with her fork. "Retired from the Air Force. Makes custom furniture."

Another jolt, with a memory attached, something she'd forgotten over the years. "Woodworking," Kim murmured. The tiny, smooth, sleeping dog.

She didn't remember getting rid of it. Maybe it was in a box somewhere. She'd replaced it with a series of worry stones, one of which she still carried.

Another lifetime, she thought.

"So, are you going to meet him?" she asked.

"We've talked about it, and I'd like to, but I wanted to run it by you first."

"Sweetheart, I'm happy that you can have the chance to get to know him. I'm not sure how I'd feel about you inviting him to the wedding, but other than that…"

Amber laughed again. "No worries there. I just want to get to know him, unless he turns out to be an ass."

"He won't," Kim said before she even had time to think. But the statement felt right. The Kevin she remembered had been kind, respectful, funny. Like her back then, he just hadn't been a fully formed adult yet.

She poked her spoon into another ice cream ball. The ice cream was soft inside its shell, but tasted just fine.

Of course she'd been curious to hear how Amber's meeting with Kevin went—Amber had driven up to Tacoma the following weekend to have lunch with him—but she didn't expect Amber to say, "He'd like to meet up with you, too, if you're okay with that. He says he has something to tell you."

Amber said he hadn't elaborated, and Kim finally decided it was just to say sorry. She was probably being a *tiniest* bit petty by making him come to her, but he'd been the one to leave in the first place, right?

She lived in the Portland suburb of Beaverton, a city largely made up of strip malls and housing for people who couldn't afford to live downtown or who wanted actual yards. Her own house was at the end of a cul-de-sac and surrounded by moss-covered pines, making it feel much more secluded from the neighbors than it actually was. It bordered a tree-filled park on one side, where she went for daily walks with her dogs.

Now she waited in a nearby Starbucks. She'd wanted a neutral spot. They'd have coffee, chat, the end.

So why was she more jittery than a cat trying to cover up poop on a marble floor? Why was her stomach in knots?

She'd ordered a green tea Frappuccino because it was a beautiful spring day. The sun was shining, which wasn't as rare as outsiders thought. (Let them think it rained all the time. Enough people were relocating to Oregon as it was.) But she was too nervous to take more than a few sips.

The coffee shop was about half-full, and most of those people were typing on laptops or immersed in their phones. Smooth, forgettable jazz was the music choice of the day.

She'd taken forever to decide where to sit—finally deciding on two brown leather armchairs off to one side against the windows, so they'd have a little privacy, but not so tucked away that he'd have trouble finding her—and she felt silly for over-thinking it.

Let's not get started on how long it had taken to pick her outfit. She'd settled on skinny jeans with a bit of stretch in them (Amber would probably call them "mom jeans," but she'd get to the age where comfort won out over fashion), and a floaty shirt with a dark red and cream floral pattern that showed just a hint of cleavage. Enough makeup to look pulled together.

She wanted to look good. Not in a "look how hot I am; aren't you sorry now?" sort of way, but in a "I'm happy and confident with my life; how are you?" sort of way.

At least she'd resisted texting Amber with pictures of various outfit choices.

A woman with a happy, tail-wagging Husky went by the window, and Kim smiled, watching them. When she looked back at the front door, a man was standing there, gazing around the room as if looking for someone.

He looked different, yes, but with a stomach-thumping twist, she *knew*.

He had the precise bearing and straight spine of an ex-military man, even in his casual jeans and green chambray button-down shirt. He *had* gone bald, mostly. What was left was shorn close, and he wore a brown leather newsboy-style cap. To her surprise, it suited him. His face was leaner now, the cheekbones sharper, and he looked...*good*. Better. The boy had been cute. The man was *handsome*.

His gaze landed on her, the question left his eyes to be replaced by recognition, and he smiled.

That smile had always done her in, and now she really saw both the boy and the man he'd become. The smile was the same, wide and genuine even though at this moment there was a hint of something else in it.

He started towards her, and as she stood, she recognized what it was.

He was just as nervous as she was.

"Kim," he said. "Wow, you... I'd've recognized you anywhere. You look great."

"Hi," she said, and stopped, because she wasn't sure what to say next. She started to raise her arms to hug him, realized that was probably far too intimate, and dropped them just as he stuck out his hand, then pulled it back, no doubt thinking that was too formal.

They both laughed the embarrassed laugh that people do when they're trying to pass each other but keep shifting in the same direction.

"It's good to see you," she said.

"You, too," he said. He slipped off his brown leather jacket, draped it over the arm of the easy chair, and said, "Can I get you anything?"

She nodded at her drink. "I'm fine, thanks." Still courteous. Nice to see.

She sat and watched him order, chatting comfortably with the barista as he handed over cash and dropped the change in the clear plastic tip jar.

He came back, sat, and shifted a bit before leaning forward a little.

"Thanks for seeing me," he said. "When Amber pinged me on Facebook...wow, I was blown away. I'm...I'm really glad to get to know her. She seems like an amazing woman."

"She is," Kim said, unable to keep the pride out of her voice. "She impresses me every day."

"You did a good job, obviously," he said.

"No matter what, she was my number-one priority," Kim said. "Her stepdad did a lot, too."

He nodded, rubbed a hand over his chin.

"Amber says you have three kids?" Kim asked.

He smiled again, and it brightened his face.

(Brightened the room, she thought, unbidden. Then she wondered what the hell she was thinking.)

"Two boys and a girl," he said. "They're great kids. Billy—he's the youngest—just graduated from U-Dub."

Amber had told her that she was looking forward to meeting them. Kevin had told the three about her and they were excited about having a half-sister.

Kevin said he and his ex had grown apart, and when Billy hit college, they'd drifted even further, without the kids to glue them together. It had been an amicable divorce, though, to the point that they'd laughed so much together at their eldest son's wedding a few months ago that people were surprised they weren't still a couple. "We're friends," he said. "The spark just went away."

The barista called his name, and he got up to retrieve his coffee. When he returned, he took a swallow, then set it on the table.

"You know," he said carefully, "for a long time, I was really mad at you, Kim."

"At me?" She blinked, surprised. Whatever she'd been expecting, it hadn't been that. "What did I do?"

He chewed on his lip. "Amber said you never heard from me."

"I told you I was pregnant, you said we'd figure things out

so I could go to Oklahoma with you, and then…you were gone." She said it without bitterness; it was just what had happened.

He shook his head slightly. "When she told me…God, it all suddenly made sense. I called your house, but your parents always answered. I came by before I shipped out, but they asked me to leave. And I wrote to you, so many times… but all the letters were returned."

"What? I never got any letters from you."

His lips thinned. "That's what Amber said. Fact is, I wrote to you at least once a week for a year. I was miserable in Oklahoma, and I missed you so much…I couldn't understand why you didn't answer."

Kim pressed a hand to her mouth as he spoke. "My parents," she whispered. "I was in Florida, and my parents returned all the letters from you."

He nodded. "After Amber told me, I called my mom—she now admits she tossed the letters you sent."

"But why?" Kim asked, and even as she asked it, she knew the answer.

"You were sixteen, and smart, and had your whole life ahead of you," he said, "and I was a high school dropout and a lowly Airman. That's what your parents saw. My parents… well, my mom said they didn't want me to get tied down with a wife and kid before I knew what I really wanted, but honestly, I wouldn't be surprised if they did it out of spite. I was the first one in my family to get away and make something of myself."

That was the difference with their parents, Kim knew. Her own parents hadn't had much—they'd lived in a trailer park and most of her clothes had come from Goodwill until she got a summer job at fourteen at one of the farm stands nearby—but they'd believed in her and what she could do with her life.

"They wanted to protect me," she said. "Obviously I don't agree with their decision, but in hindsight, I understand why they did what they did. They were embarrassed about my getting pregnant, but they supported my decision to keep Amber, at least. I'm sorry about your family, and what you went through. You know, it always impressed me how you turned their negativity around and used it as the impetus to better yourself."

His generous mouth quirked in a half-grin. "Thank you," he said. "I ended up taking the tests and becoming an officer. Retired as a Captain."

"Good for you!" Kim said. "How'd you end up in Tacoma?"

"My final station was McChord," he said. "My wife liked it, my kids were in high school and didn't want to move, and it reminded me of upstate New York, only without the crazy winters."

Kim laughed. "I thought I never wanted to go through those winters again, and then my parents sent me to live with my aunt in Florida when I was pregnant, and it was *awful*. I thought it would be beaches and palm trees, but it was muggy and full of old people."

She told him how she'd come to Portland for her husband's work, and had a similar reaction to how he'd viewed Tacoma. Because he asked, she went back in time to recount how she'd gotten her GED, gone to junior college for years at night until she had enough credits for an Associate's Degree, and gone on to double major in Accounting and English Lit.

And they just kept talking, about everything and nothing, catching up on the past thirty years and the lives they'd led. When they got around to talking about dogs—she had two mutts, Bender and Standish, and he had a Golden Retriever named Casey—Kim finally noticed that it had gotten dark. They'd been talking for hours.

"I really have to go," she said. "They have a doggy door, but I still like to take them for a walk every day."

"And I've got a drive ahead of me," Kevin said. He picked up her long-empty cup along with his and dropped them both in the trash before shrugging into his coat. He hesitated, then turned to her, standing so close she could smell the leather of his jacket.

"It really has been wonderful reconnecting with you, Kim," he said. "I'm glad we got to clear things up about what happened. I hope you know I never would have abandoned you like that."

"I know," she said. "And I would never have shut you out or kept you away from your daughter. I'm glad she has the chance to know her father now."

"You know, Amber's coming up to Tacoma in a few weeks to meet my kids—we're going to barbeque if the weather's nice," he said. "I'd love it if you could come, too."

She realized she'd been reluctant to say good-bye, and the thought of seeing him again warmed her. She was glad to discover she still liked him after all these years.

So, now, it was natural to hug him good-bye.

She was surprised that she felt safe in his arms, just as she had all those years ago.

It felt good. Really good.

She didn't have to wait a few weeks to reconnect with him. When she texted him to ask if there was anything she could bring to the barbeque, she told herself it was just to be polite. When he called to tell her how much he was enjoying a book she'd recommended, she told herself he was just being friendly.

When she felt sixteen again, giddy at the idea of seeing him again, on the drive up to Tacoma with Amber, she told herself she was just being silly.

Silly, she thought again when he opened the door and saw his face break into that smile, and her heart gave just the tiniest jolt.

His ranch-style house overlooked a lake, with a terraced redwood deck leading down to a sloping green lawn, and was filled with his custom furniture, sleek lines and gentle curves and Eastlake-inspired turned legs. She liked his kids—Billy, Cole, and Jaime, who was pregnant with her first child—and Amber was right: they were thrilled to meet their half-sister.

If she'd thought the situation would feel weird, meeting her baby daddy's other kids, she was wrong; everyone made her feel at home. What was weird was when Kevin's ex, Melinda, stopped by with a bottle of wine, eager to meet Amber as well...but then, within a quarter of an hour, Kim felt comfortable with her, too.

"We are all the most adulting of adults I've ever met," she commented.

Kevin flipped a sizzling burger (he was grilling the onion slices, too, and everything smelled amazing) and said, "We could be our own reality show."

"Too boring because we all get along," Kim said. "We'd never get ratings unless we screamed and threw things at each other."

Melinda didn't stay for food, saying she had another party to get to. When she left, she punched Kim gently in the arm and said, low enough so nobody else would hear, "Don't let him get away again."

Kim sputtered, but Melinda was already headed out the door.

But Melinda's words got her thinking….

No, that wasn't true. She'd already been thinking.

She'd always thought of herself as pragmatic, a problem solver…at least, once she'd given birth, which had made her grow up a whole hell of a lot. She'd targeted goals and hit them: GED, college, career, all while raising the best daughter she could.

Over the years, though, more than one person had referred to her as a hopeless romantic. She'd always laughed that away. And now? Seriously, she was approaching middle age. Romance was for the young.

But she'd been young when she thought she was in love with Kevin. A teenaged, puppy love.

Could she be in love with him again? Could that first, naïve love have held a grain of truth, the seeds for a mature connection?

She wasn't the girl she'd been then. Kevin wasn't that boy, either. They'd grown and changed, matured, lived. Yet… Kevin the man, containing the core of the boy he'd been, was proving to be pretty freaking awesome.

A few days later, Kim got a letter from Kevin in the mail.

All of my previous letters were returned, it said in part, *so I thought I'd try one more time.*

Although they were making use of the various forms of connection they hadn't had thirty years ago—texting, friending on another on Facebook, and even Skyping—the handwritten note charmed her.

The letter, and everything it represented.

Of course she wrote back. And signed her name as she had back then, with a heart dotting the I.

Then he texted her to say he was going to be in Portland to deliver some furniture, and could they get together? She agreed, but when she suggested a restaurant, he responded with "Let me surprise you."

The address he gave her was for an Indian restaurant in a strip mall, which wasn't that much of a surprise. She wasn't sure, as she pulled into the parking lot, whether she felt disappointed.

That changed when she saw him waiting by his truck. It was a gorgeous day, sunny but not too warm, and he wore the faded jeans he wore so well, and a red T-shirt, and his newsboy cap.

She didn't feel disappointed.

She felt a hit of adrenaline and delight course through her.

The restaurant, the surprise (or lack thereof) didn't matter.

She was wrong again.

Instead of heading to the restaurant, he took her hand and led her to the business next door. When she read the sign, she burst out laughing.

"Glow-in-the-dark mini putt?"

"Mini putt was our main form of entertainment in Plattsburgh that summer, as I recall," he said.

And it had been. She'd go to the fairy-tale-themed park with her friends, where they'd all meet up with their boyfriends. Cheaper than the movies, the mini putt arcade also provided beach access to the lake, so they'd spend the day swimming, sunbathing, and attempting to make par on every hole, even the weird one where you had to shoot through a witch's hat.

They entered the lobby, to be greeted with what looked like one of the creatures from the *Alien* movies.

"I thought our main form of entertainment back then had been sex," she joked.

He squeezed her hand. "I wasn't aware that was an option."

The thought had crossed her mind once or twice. Or more. "Depends on whether you let me win," she said.

"Darlin', I never let you win. You were frighteningly good at mini putt."

They went through the glass doors into the main part of the arcade. It was dark, with glowing lights on the ceiling. Ahead of them was the counter, with a row of putters lined up on it and a rack of golf balls in neon colors: hot pink, chartreuse, turquoise, lime green. To their left, a line of video game machines pinged and bonged, and "Broken Wings" by Mr. Mister, one of her favorite songs from the eighties, played over the sound system.

Kim would've liked the place for the music alone, but being here with Kevin, preparing to have a completely random game of mini putt while giant mutant bees loomed over them (hole 3) or slugs the size of beagles (hole 6, around the corner), was just sublime.

She loved that he'd remembered their mini putt dates from thirty years ago. She loved that he'd taken the time to find this place. She loved that it was two o'clock on a Saturday afternoon and she had a date with…

"Hold on," she said as he handed her a club and grabbed a pencil and scorecard. "Is this a date?"

He bounced his bright blue ball in his hand. "Do you want it to be?"

"Yes." Yes, she did.

"Oh, good," he said, "because that's what it's supposed to be."

The only other players, a foursome, were seven or eight holes ahead of them, so it felt like they had the place to themselves. Between the music and the noises that some of the holes made (like one that had what looked like a metal-barred door that half-opened and then banged shut while something behind it moaned), she couldn't hear the people ahead of them anyway.

Kevin cheered when she hit a completely accidental hole-in-one on the second hold, which involved hitting the ball into a tunnel. He didn't rib her too much when his shot on the next hole completely blocked her perfect line-up to the hole.

She hummed along to Heart's "These Dreams," and then the next song that came on was "Don't You Forget About Me."

She stopped in mid-swing, straightened.

"The music," she said.

"Yes?" he said. Even in the half-light, she could see him trying not to smile.

"This is the mix tape you made for me."

He failed, and grinned. "Yep."

"How did you…?"

"I have my ways." He waggled his eyebrows, and Kim melted. Just utterly melted.

He'd set this all up perfectly.

"Next you're going to tell me you carved me another little wooden dog."

"In the truck. And there are two. Thanks for posting lots of pictures of Bender and Standish on Facebook."

She propped her putter against a faux crate painted neon yellow and black, then stepped into his arms, wrapping hers around him. "So, is this date going to end like our old ones did?"

"I certainly hope so," he said. "Although with any luck it'll include a real bed, not the back of my truck."

"Good," she said. "Just so you know, I'm on the pill."

She felt his chest move as he laughed softly. "Good to know. I have a box of condoms, too."

Their chuckles faded as they gazed at one another. Kevin smoothed a lock of hair away from her face.

"I missed you, Kim," he said. "You broke my heart like nobody could, and though I've had a great life, I like my life a hell of a lot more now that you're back in it."

"You broke my heart, too," she said. "But I trust you not to do it again."

The kiss was like the first time all over again. Their second first kiss, and their second chance for love.

LEAVE A CANDLE BURNING

She was lost.

Claudia stopped in the tree-lined lane, surrounded by the deep blue of twilight, a swirl of snowflakes, and an ever-growing drift of snow on the ground, and shook her head at her own stupidity.

In truth, the lodge she was heading for (at least, she hoped she was heading in the right direction) wasn't far from the train station. Walking normally wouldn't have been a problem. She just hadn't factored in the earlier sunset this far north and the fact that it might be snowing.

Snowing, right before Christmas, in upstate New York? Not all that shocking.

Thankfully, her job scouting for a TV show meant she knew how to pack light—at least she wasn't dragging a suitcase behind her. She wore her bulky winter coat and boots, and everything else, including laptop, camera, and clothes, were in her backpack. She'd had to hike to sites before.

Just not in the damn snow.

The world held that silent quality that came only in the winter. The snow padded the ground, muffled the air. All she could hear was her own breathing, and the occasional, tiny snap of a twig as some small animal settled for the night.

The birch trees' pale bark glowed in the moonlight.

Claudia felt like she stood in the middle of a snow globe.

She thought she'd walked the two miles already, but nary a house was in sight, not even a glow of lights. She didn't think the snow would have knocked out the power, so this was worrying. The GPS on her phone had been no help: the small dirt lanes didn't register on the map. And then, of course, because she'd spent too much time on the train working, her battery had died. She couldn't even call.

She was just about to turn around and head back to the station when she caught motion out of the corner of her eye. She hadn't heard anyone approach; her own gasp sounded loud against the sudden pounding of her heart.

Not a someone...a something. A large white dog—a husky or a white German shepherd, it was hard to tell in the dark—stood a few feet away, tail waving languidly, tongue out, watching her.

"Well, hello there, pup," she said in a soothing tone, holding out her hand flat. "Where did you come from?"

The dog barked, and jerked its head in a gesture that looked suspiciously like *Come on, then*. It took a few steps towards the trees, then looked back expectantly.

Its message was clear: *Follow me*.

Seriously?

The dog came back a few steps and barked again, this time more impatiently, then turned and looked over its shoulder.

The dog could be leading her to shelter, Claudia supposed. Or it could be leading her to someone or something in trouble. Or it could just be leading her...no, why would the dog be trying to lead her nowhere? Even if it wasn't to the lodge, it would be somewhere with a phone or a car. Dogs didn't lead people to scary shacks containing serial killers, after all.

Claudia always trusted her instincts, and they'd never proven her wrong. She also had a lot of faith in dogs. Her choice was clear.

She settled her pack more firmly on her shoulders and followed the dog into the woods.

The trees weren't closely spaced and there was no foliage beneath the snow to trip her up, although in a few open places the snow had piled up. The dog seemed to take delight in bounding off to leap through the drifts before running back to trot ahead of her.

They hadn't walked more than ten minutes when Claudia saw lights. As they drew closer, she breathed a sigh of relief, recognizing the stone-and-timber lodge from pictures. The dog had in fact led her directly to Heather Mountain Lodge.

The three-story building toed the line between Victorian and mountain rustic. The roof was steeply pitched to keep too much snow from collecting, with two levels of dormers and multiple chimneys dotting the expanse.

Warm lights glowed from multiple windows, bathing the snow in warm, welcoming gold, a gorgeous contrast to the midnight blue sky and gleaming snow. Fairy lights in the bare trees added to the cheer. Claudia felt warmer already.

Home. In an odd way, that's what it felt like, even though Claudia had never been here before. She'd grown up in the northeast, though, and the scene was familiar enough.

Plus, her tiny apartment—the tradeoff for a nice place in LA was size—had never felt homey, and now she'd been told that due to budget cuts, she was expected to telecommute.

She sighed, blowing out the melancholy. She'd worry about that after the holidays. Right now, she had a job to do.

"Good job, pup!" she said. The dog barked one more time

and trotted away, around the building. Probably a doggie door in the back, leading to a mud room or kitchen.

She went up the flagstone steps to the enclosed porch that ran the length of the building and let herself in, stomping her feet on the entry rug to knock off the snow before continuing to the front door.

Before she could ring the bell, she saw movement through the glass, and then the door opened.

"You must be Claudia," the very attractive man said. His eyes were the same deep blue as the winter twilight she'd just hiked through, and his welcoming smile sparkled in those eyes like snow under moonlight.

Something tugged at her, deep in her core. It was like the sensation she'd felt when she'd seen the lodge. *Home.*

But that made no sense—tall-dark-and-handsome shouldn't evoke *home*. *Instant lust*, maybe (and there was that, too), but not *home*.

"Must I?" she asked cheekily, stepping inside.

"Mrs. Hawley said someone named Claudia was supposed to arrive tonight, and she's been fretting that you're late and your phone goes straight to voicemail," he said, his voice low and pleasant. He closed the door. "So it's a good assumption you're Claudia."

"Excellent powers of deduction," Claudia said, holding out her gloved hand.

"Excellent powers of being Claudia," he said, shaking her hand. "I'm Reese. D'you mind leaving your boots on the porch?"

She saw the row of winter footwear lined up next to a rough-hewn bench. Dropping her pack next to her, she sat to unlace her hiking boots.

She sensed, rather than saw, Reese lean comfortably against the doorjamb. A glance showed he'd tucked his hands in his pockets.

"Do you work here?" she asked.

"No. I was on my way back from the bathroom when I saw you on the porch. But I grew up nearby, so I'm familiar with the place."

She stood in her thick socks, and saw him grin. Thought she saw the flash of a dimple, even.

"And I figured," he went on, scooping up her pack for her, "here's my chance to meet this intriguing latecomer before anyone else. Good thing I trusted my instincts. Come on in," he added, stepping aside to let her enter. "Mrs. Hawley's in the parlor with some of the other guests."

It was warm inside, enough to make her chilled cheeks hurt in a pleasant way—although she had to admit it wasn't the only reason her cheeks were flushed. She shivered, adjusting to the change in temperature.

She followed Reese through the foyer, unable to decide whether to look at the gorgeous architecture or him (also gorgeous). The foyer, although paneled with dark wood, was welcoming thanks to the warm light from antique Tiffany lamps and the faded oriental rug covering the center of the floor. A steep staircase dominated the right side, its likely hand-carved newel posts a testament to an art form mostly lost today. The wood—currently wrapped with a sweet-smelling pine garland—shone, polished by more than a century of hands caressing the railing as residents and then hotel guests made their way up- or downstairs.

Claudia smiled, feeling the tension melt away. She already liked it here.

She had a job to do, so she shouldn't allow herself to be distracted by Reese, but unfortunately, she already was. Okay, maybe not full-on *attracted to* after their extremely brief conversation, but at least *appreciative of.*

The snug way his jeans hugged him didn't hurt, definitely. Nor did the in-need-of-a-trim black hair, striking blue eyes, and warm smile. Nor the comfortable way he led her through to the parlor. Not cocky, but simply confident, settled in his own skin.

She wouldn't have minded more time alone with him, but there were other people in the parlor, and that settled that.

"Oh goodness," said a tall, rangy older woman, "you must be Claudia."

"I must," she agreed this time. "You're Mrs. Hawley?"

"That I am." The woman's white hair framed a face that showed a lifetime of smiles in the fine lines around her eyes and mouth. "Let me show you to your room, dearie, and then you can settle in and meet folks. Shall I make you a pot of tea? Or hot chocolate? Or…?"

"Hot chocolate sounds lovely," Claudia said. She leaned in conspiratorially. "Especially if it has a nip of crème de menthe in it."

Mrs. Hawley smiled. "Absolutely," she said.

"This is perfect," Claudia said when she saw her room. The turned-wood four-poster bed had a cream-colored, crocheted blanket at its foot and a lavender-scented sachet on the pillow, and the room's uneven wooden floors creaked as she entered. Cozy and charming. "I'll be down in a few minutes."

It took her even less than that—the lingering chill (although the room itself was toasty) drove her to drop her backpack and shuck her parka before plugging in her traitorous phone and heading downstairs to properly meet the rest of the guests.

Back in the parlor, she was happy to settle in an antique sofa near the stone fireplace, where a fire crackled and spat heat and the scent of wood smoke. Happy especially because the free spot was next to Reese.

"Mrs. Hawley's off making your hot chocolate; we had an early supper so she could let the cook go for the night because of the snow," Reese said. "Which doesn't bode well for breakfast."

"We aren't going to be snowed in for long, I hope?" asked a man wearing glasses and a Dr. Horrible T-shirt, who'd been introduced as Matt. He held hands with a pretty redhead—Holly—wearing multicolored striped socks and a matching crocheted hat.

"The weather report said it should stop snowing overnight," said a teenaged girl with a blond French braid, glancing up from her phone. Brittany, Claudia repeated to herself. Her parents, Tom and Sherry, had already gone upstairs, as had the final guest, Angela, a musician.

"And once the plow comes through, we'll be fine," Reese added.

Mrs. Hawley returned with Claudia's hot chocolate, and now that this crop of guests was assembled, began her story.

"The White Lady," Mrs. Hawley said, settling herself into her chair and into her story. "We don't know much about who she was when she was alive, but we know this: She was married, and her husband was away one night in late December. I've heard different stories—that he'd been out hunting that day, that he went out in the storm to help someone. As the snow came down harder, she knew it would be more difficult for her husband to find his way home. So she went from window to window, lighting candles to guide him to safety."

Mrs. Hawley paused to take a sip of her own hot chocolate before continuing.

"Since then, each year, starting a day or two before Christmas and going until a day or two afterwards, after dusk falls she moves through the lower rooms of the house, lighting candles in the windows to bring her beloved home."

Holly shivered. "That's a beautiful story." She squeezed Matt's hand. "So romantic."

Romantic, yes, but whether there was any truth to the story…well, that was Claudia's job to figure out.

"What style of clothing does she wear?" she asked. "A nightgown? A Victorian dress? Earlier period, later?"

"Oh, well, I can't say for sure," Mrs. Hawley said, looking down at her hands. "I'm not an expert in these things."

"I understand," Claudia said. "It's just, if we can narrow down her clothing style, we can narrow down who she might be."

"Oh, that's right," Reese said, turning toward her in interest. Claudia felt that flutter in her stomach again at hearing his mellow voice. "You're from one of those reality shows— you're a ghost hunter."

Claudia laughed, glad that he seemed to be taking her seriously. "Not hardly. I'm a location scout; I don't get any air time at all. And *America's Legendary Ghosts* isn't a ghost-hunting show—we don't run around with EMF detectors or try to debunk the stories. We focus on the truth behind the legend…we want to know whether the ghost story has some basis in history. We're more of a history program than a reality show."

"So you're here to decide whether The White Lady is real or not?" Holly asked.

Claudia reluctantly turned her gaze away from Reese. "I'm here to discover whether there's any historical basis for The White Lady," she explained. Then, to Mrs. Hawley, she added, "I assume you've seen her?"

"Indeed I have." Mrs. Hawley sat up straight. "Every year."

"Please, tell me."

"We've had candles in the windows here in winter for as

long as I can remember—and I've been here since I was a little girl. Even if no one sees her, people come down in the morning and find candles burning, or melted wax where the candles have burned down."

"And what happens if people try to interact with her?" Claudia asked.

"They can't," Mrs. Hawley said. "She doesn't respond to any attempts to communicate with her. If people come close, she disappears."

"Vanishes?" Claudia clarified.

"Essentially."

"Did her husband make it home?" Matt asked.

Mrs. Hawley looked sad. "We don't know," she said. "We just don't know."

"I'm guessing he didn't," Claudia said. "If he had, she wouldn't feel compelled to keep lighting the candles."

They all stared at her as if she'd just kicked their collective puppy. Clearly she'd harshed their mellow. What had they expected? Before she had a chance to speak, Brittany looked up from her phone and said, "Well, isn't it *obvious*? It's a *ghost*. It's not supposed to be *happy*."

Although the others nodded in agreement, that effectively killed the conversation. After one or two more half-hearted questions, the group broke up, Mrs. Hawley retiring for an early night so she could handle breakfast.

"You didn't get any supper, did you?" Reese asked Claudia.

She'd been so intent on learning about the ghost that she hadn't realized until now that she was starving, and she appreciated him realizing she might not have eaten. She had a power bar in her luggage, but the hell with that. Any extra time she could spend with him was a bonus, and if he could point her towards food....

"I had a snack on the train, but that was it," she said.

"Come with me."

She followed him to the kitchen—both because she didn't know where it was and because it was an opportunity to ogle his butt again in those faded, snug jeans.

The kitchen had been upgraded with professional appliances, but still held the sense of a homey Victorian kitchen, thanks to details such as herbs drying from a rack hanging from the ceiling, a fireplace with a bread oven along one wall, and an open wooden cabinet displaying blue-patterned china.

"You said you used to live here?" Claudia asked. "Mrs. Hawley seems comfortable with you."

"I grew up in the area," Reese said. He stripped off his sweater, and she caught a flash of taut abs dusted with dark hair as the T-shirt beneath rode up. Yummy. She fumbled herself onto a barstool, but he didn't notice, being too busy opening cabinets and pulling out a plate and bread with a comfortable ease, as if he were well acquainted with the layout. "My mom worked for Mrs. Hawley for a few years, so I hung out here a lot. I'd like to say I was helping, but I'm pretty sure I was just underfoot."

"I grew up in Albany, actually," Claudia said. "I've never been here, but I've been to Lake Placid a few times."

"Not too far away, then," Reese said. "Welcome back."

So different from the men she'd met in California, she mused. It wasn't that nobody was nice there, but she did work in Hollywood, after all. Everybody seemed to be angling for something—and seemed to be made of hard edges. Reese seemed confident, but in a comfortable way; like he was settled in his own skin.

Maybe that was the familiarity and comfort that tugged at her.

Claudia propped her elbows on the butcher block island. "So, have you seen The White Lady?"

"As a matter of fact, I have." He was leaning into the industrial refrigerator, so she couldn't see his face, although his deep voice was casual and self-assured. He didn't sound like he was lying. "I was walking by the parlor and I saw her in there. It scared the snot out of me, and I ran to find my mom."

He emerged from the fridge, balancing ham and cheese and condiments in his arms. Claudia held her breath until the food was safely deposited on the butcher block. She felt bad for not helping, but damn, she was tired.

"We moved the year after that," he went on. "Late summer. So I never had the chance to see her again."

"Is that why you've come back?"

He turned away to find a knife, turned back. "No, not really. I…my folks are both gone, and my brother and sister were off doing their own thing, so I just wanted to come back and recapture the fond memories." He handed her the knife and shoved the condiments across the island. "What about you? It must suck to work on Christmas."

She opened the jar of stone-ground mustard, spread some on the wheat bread. "Kinda. My family's big, and we decided a few years ago to make Thanksgiving the big holiday—my folks are in Florida now, and we rotate between locations—and we're on our own for Christmas."

More than *kinda*, she'd realized on the hike here, but she wanted to keep the conversation positive. No sense scaring a guy away by immediately admitting that you can't hold down a relationship because your job requires you to travel so much. Her last boyfriend finally up and decided that didn't work for him.

Oddly, it had worked for her. Oh, he hadn't been a bad guy—she thought she'd loved him, eaten an awful lot of Ben & Jerry's after his departure—but the fact was, she loved to travel and loved the chance to be on her own. Absence did make the heart grow fonder, at least for her.

Unfortunately, not many people shared that view, and constant travel made it hard to even get to know someone long enough to find out if they shared that view.

Claudia added ham, Swiss, and tomato slices to her sandwich, and continued focusing on the positive. "Being free on Christmas gives me a little more leeway—you'd be surprised how many ghost legends revolve around the holidays."

"Maybe Dickens was on to something."

She laughed. "Maybe so. There certainly haven't been any Thanksgiving ghosts for us." She put some baby spinach on the sandwich, covered it with a second slice of bread, and pressed down with both hands to smoosh it down to a more comfortable height. "I'm just glad I'm here this year. It's always depressing to be without snow on Christmas. Despite what the rest of Hollywood likes, I don't want to be wearing shorts in December. It's just *wrong*."

"I hear you," Reese said. "One year I was in Australia for Christmas. The big heavy Christmas dinner makes no sense when it's a bazillion degrees out." He was already tidying away the sandwich fixings.

"What took you there?" Claudia took a big bite of her sandwich, stifling a moan of pleasure. She hadn't realized she was *that* hungry. Maybe it was the crème de menthe talking.

"I'm a structural engineer, specializing in earthquake retrofits," he said. "I was working on a government contract."

Now that she had a little food in her (that wasn't sugar laced with alcohol), she was able to focus again. She found herself distracted by his hands, competently wiping down the butcher block.

Thought about those hands on her body.

She was tired, but she wasn't *that* tired.

"Does your job take you all over?" she asked, because dragging him down on the butcher block and having her way with him might be a tiny bit too forward.

"Everywhere there are earthquakes, which is as all over as you can get," he said.

"And where do you live when you're not wandering the globe?"

"I've got an apartment in the city, but it's mostly a place to store my stuff. I'm thinking about—"

They heard a shout, and then Holly appeared in the kitchen doorway. "Come quick!" she said. "We've seen The White Lady!"

Claudia dropped the second half of her sandwich and bolted for the foyer, Reese on her heels. When they arrived, the rest of the guests were there, in various stages of settling in: Angela was in a flowered flannel nightgown, with a matching robe belted firmly around her, while Tom's wet hair suggested he'd been in the shower.

"In the parlor, where we were earlier," Holly said.

Sure as shooting, the candles in the window had been lit, a smudge of wax on the windowsill indicating someone had bumped the candle after it had been burning.

"Candles," Claudia said. "Did anyone see The White Lady?"

"I did," Matt said, raising his hand. "I came back down to get my phone, and there she was. She vanished before I got into the room."

"Vanished how?" Claudia asked. She didn't want to sound suspicious; hated ruining the other guests' excitement. Even as she spoke, she felt the energy in the room drop.

"Just...I don't know, exactly." Matt looked abashed. "I turned to call up the stairs to Holly, and when I turned back, the Lady was gone. But I know she didn't go past me."

The parlor's only other door led to the dining room, and the door between the dining room and the kitchen had been open—surely she and Reese would have heard someone in there?

Claudia asked a few more questions, then decided not to investigate tonight. There would be time for that in the morning.

Time to figure out if this was a legend worth pursuing... and if Reese was, as well.

Nah. She'd already decided that he was. But exhaustion was crowding out interest, and she still had a job to do.

Dammit.

Claudia shoved the drapes aside and smiled at the sun sparkling on the fresh, untouched snow.

A good night's sleep under cozy flannel sheets and a warm down comforter had gone a long way to improving her outlook on life. The snow had been hauntingly lovely last night, but she'd been lost and cold and hungry; today, she could simply appreciate its beauty. She wondered how the dog was doing, and made a mental note to ask Mrs. Hawley.

The dining room had a big stone fireplace and large windows that looked out on the mountains. Quiet holiday music filled the background from unseen speakers.

Even better, the dining room had Reese in it.

And when she saw him, she had that same damn curious tug at her very core.

She said good morning to him, as well as Brittany, her parents, and Angela, who were the only other ones there, then helped herself to food from the sideboard. She slid into the seat catty-corner from Reese, wanting to watch him without being obvious. But from the way he smiled at her, she suspected he'd notice, because he'd be watching her, too.

His smile made her feel all melty, like an icicle in the sun. Damn, what was happening to her?

"This is just lovely," Sherry enthused. "I've always wanted to get away for Christmas. And I love the decorations."

"They're beautiful," Claudia agreed. "My apartment's way to small for a tree, and I travel so much that decorating seems more like clutter-adding than something festive."

Reese asked, "Well, then, what's your favorite part about Christmas?"

"Ideally, I love the ritual of it all," Claudia confessed. "Trimming the tree, wrapping the presents, sitting down for dinner with family…"

"And snow," Reese said with a wink that said he remembered their conversation from the night before. "Don't forget about the snow."

"But you can have the rituals without snow," Tom said.

Claudia had almost forgotten there were other people at the table.

"That's true," Reese said. "Claudia's right: It's about being with family and friends—rituals are about sharing the same joys with the people you love."

Everyone murmured assent, and then they all started discussing their rituals and childhood memories: tinsel versus garland, holly and mistletoe, favorite carols. And cookies. The cookie debate almost got a little heated.

Claudia, who didn't even like to bake, found herself wanting to make holiday cookies with Reese. Preferably with each of them wearing little more than an apron. He'd look adorable with flour on his nose. And wearing little more than an apron.

After breakfast, Reese asked, "What's your plan for today, ghost hunter?"

"Legend hunter, please," Claudia said, cradling her hands around her coffee mug. "I'm headed into town to meet with the county clerk to look at the lodge's records, and hit the local library for their archives."

He offered to drive her, and she happily took him up on it. She could have walked, but it wouldn't be a bad idea to make sure she knew the way first. Bonus: His truck had four-wheel drive and snow tires. The driveway had already been plowed, as had the lane, but it was still a bit slippery.

Claudia laughed at herself. The truth was, she was thrilled to have the opportunity to spend more time with him.

She hadn't even been here a day, and yet she was feeling something shifting, deep, like thick ice on a river just before it breaks free.

The drive reminded her to ask Mrs. Hawley about the dog. She hadn't seen it around today, so maybe it didn't live at the lodge, but at a nearby farm.

At the county courthouse, she waded through land and tax records, making photocopies of what she needed. By the time she was done, it was lunchtime, and she met Reese, who'd been running errands, at a local restaurant.

The proprietors had gone for a full-on log cabin feel, with exposed-log walls, a pot-bellied stove, deer heads on the wall, and a taxidermied black bear to greet her at the door.

Reese had arrived before her, and was already at a table with a steaming cup of coffee, his olive parka slung over the back of his chair. A second cup of coffee sat at her place.

"I remembered you had coffee this morning, but not what you put in it," he said, pushing creamer and sugar in her direction.

The gesture warmed her more than the heat inside the diner did.

His dark hair was mussed, either from having his hood up earlier or because he'd run his fingers through it. Either way, it worked on him, and Claudia wondered if it was soft, and how it would feel to run her own fingers through it. Then draw his face towards hers...

She turned her attention to the menu, made a random decision about food because she was thinking more about how Reese's lips would feel on hers, and put the menu back down.

She wasn't used to such instant attraction, not like this. She believed herself savvy enough to get a good sense of a person early on, but when it came to relationships, the process had always been gradual. *I like you, hm, maybe I'm interested, I wonder if...*

Physical attraction, sure. But this deeper tug, this feeling of things clicking into place?

Was it the holidays? The nostalgia for proper winter? Her dissatisfaction with the place she barely called home?

She realized Reese was watching her with those winter-twilight eyes, and answered her own questions. No, it wasn't any of those things. It was this. It was him, whether she was used to it or not.

"Everything okay?" he asked.

"Sorry," she said. "Wool-gathering." Then, before she could talk herself out of it, she added, "I'm...really glad we're able to have lunch together."

Oh, Claudia. So lame.

But he smiled and said, "Me, too. It's hard to have alone time in a house full of people, even in a house as big as the lodge."

The waitress came to take their order. When she left, the spell was momentarily broken.

"So what do you really think about The White Lady?" Reese asked after swallowing some coffee. "Is she real?"

"I want her to be," Claudia admitted. "But the bottom line for me—for my job—is whether the underlying legend is real. What about you? You saw her as a child—it wasn't a childish fantasy?"

"If she isn't real, I can't blame Mrs. Hawley for making her up," Reese said. "She's been a good source of tourism for the lodge even at other times of the year. But more than that, I believe Mrs. Hawley believes. Her own husband died of a heart attack—must be twenty years ago now—and I think she likes the idea of someone being able to guide her lover home."

"Oh." Claudia looked down at her paper placemat, which bore the history of the diner. "I didn't know that. How sad."

"Don't be sad." Reese put a hand over hers. "It was a long time ago, and I'm pretty sure she's had…friends since then. But she hasn't remarried, and I know the lodge is important to her, so…"

She caught her breath. Yes. She felt the solid, comforting warmth of his touch, felt the tug of *home*, and thought, *This. This is what I want when I stagger in after a long flight.*

And, *Well, this and a continuation of the touching until we've removed each other's clothes and…*

And, *Am I going crazy?* Her emotions were going haywire, attraction and longing and happiness and sadness ribboning together.

"I get that." Claudia gathered her feelings and her thoughts. "It's just that so many of the stories are about loss. It just wears me down sometimes."

She'd never told anyone that before. She wasn't sure if she'd even realized it until now.

"I get that, too," Reese said. "We want to find our soul-mates and have happy endings."

Claudia squinted at him, but he didn't sound like he was making fun of her. Quite the opposite, in fact: If anything, he looked wistful.

He went on. "My parents truly seemed to be happy with

each other, really seemed to be in love. I guess I want to believe that's possible for anybody." He squeezed her hand, let go, and she felt an instant, sharp pang of loss.

Thankfully the waitress chose that moment to reappear with their lunches, giving her a distraction.

The cost was reasonable and the portions hearty—and, Claudia discovered, quite tasty. Her enormous bowl of chili had a nice bite to it, warming her after the walk over from the courthouse, and the buttered cornbread melted in her mouth.

"Enough about my job," she said after a few bites. "What about you?"

"It's hard, sometimes, going in after an earthquake to assess the damage and what can be done," he said. "But I like the fact that I can make buildings safer, prevent further destruction or injury. That part is truly satisfying. And I get to meet a lot of interesting people…for a little while, anyway."

"Same here," Claudia said. "But I'm also grateful for modern technology—I Skype with my folks every few weeks."

"My sister likes to call me while she's out walking," he said. "Always multitasking. I Skype with my brother so I can see his kids—he's got three now."

"What about…" Claudia bit the bullet. "Anyone else?"

He shook his head. "No one special," he said. "It's hard to maintain a relationship given all the traveling I do."

"This probably sounds weird," he said, "and may be blowing my chances, but…I don't need to be around someone twenty-four/seven. I like having time away. Then when I'm with someone, I'm really *with* them, not taking them or our time together for granted." He gave a half-shrug, a gesture so small she almost missed it. "I know it's unusual—

I've met some pretty independent women who just didn't want that level of independence."

"Tell me about it," Claudia said. "That's why my last relationship tanked. I love my job, and everywhere it takes me, but finding someone else who understands that love…"

Suddenly self-conscious, she looked down at her half-eaten chili in the white porcelain bowl.

Reese cleared his throat, and to her relief, changed the subject. "How did you end up at the show?" he asked.

She smiled, grateful for the reprieve. "I sort of fell into it. I was the family genealogist, and I played around with cameras, and couldn't decide what to major in at college. Eventually I moved to LA with a friend who wanted to be an actress, and got a job as a PA, and…I'm good at research."

"It's a good thing to be good at," he said.

"Yeah, although my boss just realized I could be good at it anywhere," she said, and proceeded to tell him about being forced to telecommute and loathing her tiny apartment. "Of course," she concluded, "I could always just become impossibly hipster and work in coffee shops."

"I rank airports by whether or not they have free wireless and how many available outlets there are," Reese said, his mouth curving into an impossibly cute grin.

"Ditto the planes themselves," Claudia said. "Give me power at my seat and I'll fly you forever."

"And hotel rooms," Reese said, almost at the same time. "Wireless, outlets, comfortable bed…"

"Absolutely," Claudia said, thinking about comfortable beds and Reese and room service.

Their shared laughter made her feel so light and airy, like a snowflake in a swirl of wind.

~

Despite the local library being in a modern building, the older records hadn't been updated to the modern age, leaving Claudia to slog through ancient microfiches of local newspaper archives and census records in the chilly, damp windowless basement.

Still, there was something about this kind of research she loved; the chance uncovering of a mystery, the allure of discovering a treasure of information.

To her delight, Reese had come with her, and helped her by making photocopies and bringing her books on local history.

It was already dusk by the time they left, Claudia's bag stuffed full of paperwork to review over the next two days.

Everyone seemed in good spirits at dinner, and hopeful that the ghost would make another sighting. She liked the way Reese was easy with everyone, even drawing Brittany away from her phone for a conversation about technology.

Plus the venison stew, roasted vegetables, and an apple pie with locally made maple ice cream almost sent Claudia into a food coma.

Afterwards they repaired to the parlor again. Reese made a point of sitting next to Claudia on the sofa, stretching out his long, jean-clad legs towards the fire.

While the other guests played a game or read and Mrs. Hawley knitted, Claudia started in on the reams of photocopies. This was a work trip—she wasn't really on vacation, despite the holiday—but when she curled up Indian-style, her knee bumping Reese's thigh, he smiled, and so she left it there, enjoying the contact. Even if it was a distraction.

Especially if it was a distraction.

This time, it was Angela who spotted something moving in the dining room when she stood to stoke the fire. Once again, they rushed across the foyer into the other room.

"What was that?" Tom asked, and at the same time Holly

said "Was that a light outside?" and Claudia had to admit that really did look like the flicker of candle flame outside the window, although neither she nor the rest of them clearly saw a person.

"We should go check for footprints," she suggested.

Clouds obscured the stars and moon, but the ambient light from the lodge along with the flashlights Mrs. Hawley procured for them provided enough illumination to show that there were no footprints outside the dining room.

It was Brittany who spotted the white candle in the white snow, its wick blackened, showing it had been used.

They all trooped back inside, kicking snow off their boots on the porch and shivering in the warmth. Mrs. Hawley went off to make hot chocolate and hot buttered rums.

Reese waited until the others had gone and just he and Claudia were still on the porch. After the flurry of other people, it felt good to be alone with him, if only for a few moments. The light gleaming from inside haloed his dark hair in its usual messy state, and she fought the urge to tame it just so she could feel it.

"What do you think about it?" he asked.

She gave a cautious shrug, glad that she had someone she felt she could trust to bounce ideas off of. "I have to admit I saw *something*, but I can't swear it was candlelight. Finding the candle on the ground was…an interesting development, though."

"And how's the research going?"

"Nothing to confirm or deny yet, but the night is young," she said. "Mrs. Hawley gave me a book on Adirondack ghost stories that includes the legend of The White Lady…but the account was given by her father, who bought the lodge before Mrs. Hawley was born. I'm still tracing back the property records from then. I need to either find some kind of proof of a woman whose husband died around the holidays, or a very old account of the ghost, or even both." She tucked her boots beneath the bench and stood.

"No rest for the wicked?" he asked.

She laughed. "Maybe tomorrow, if I get enough work done."

"Is there anything I can do to help?" he asked, holding the door to the lodge open for her.

"I wouldn't take you away from *your* vacation, but no, at this point it's all research I need to do." She smiled, honestly feeling her next words. "But I really appreciate it."

Dammit. Why couldn't this research trip be longer? She wanted more time with him.

Maybe they'd get a blizzard and get snowed in, and they could hole up in one of their bedrooms and have Mrs. Hawley send up the dog with food like a St. Bernard…

It did snow the next day, although the flakes drifted down languidly, showing no interest in being collectively labeled a blizzard. Clearly they hadn't gotten the memo.

Still, it made Claudia's work all the more pleasant. She'd missed the feeling of curling up in a comfy sweater and thick socks by a warm fire, watching the snow outside while she read and made notes and cross-referenced things.

The room smelled of pine from the garlands and cinnamon from the arrangement on the birch side table, where a lamp with amber and glass shades shaped like calla lilies illuminated her reading.

The rest of the guests had gone out cross-country skiing, so she had the place to herself, except for the cook making their supper feast and Mrs. Hawley catching up on paperwork in her own office.

Reese had sat with her after lunch, catching up on e-mail

on his tablet. When he left with the others, he said it was to give her time to work. But the fact was, she'd been fine having him in the room. He'd respected her by staying quiet, and when she'd tossed a fact or idea at him, he'd had helpful comments.

No, she hadn't been just fine. She'd liked having him there. More than she'd expected.

The thought made her smile, kept her warm while she read and researched, stayed with her as the midnight blue of twilight fell. She poured a Scotch on the rocks and stood by the window, watching the blue-white glow of the snow and the flakes trickling down past the icicles hanging from the eaves.

She intended to curl back up with her research, but instead she picked up the brochures she'd seen on a side table, flyers listing local homes for sale.

She sat down, spread them out on the sofa, picked up each one. The pictures showed the houses in all seasons—the area was known for skiing, both downhill and cross-country, snow shoeing, ice skating, and even dogsled rides on the frozen lake. In the summer, there was hiking, swimming, boating.

She was surprised at how they made her heart wrench, just a little. What was it about a chalet-style cottage, its roof steeply pitched to slough off snow, that was just so damned charming?

In truth, she'd barely had a few sips of whiskey before she closed her eyes. Resting her head against a pillow, she listened to the soft music playing from hidden speakers: a chorale version of "Silent Night."

She thought about saving her money and buying a holiday home in the mountains.

She thought about Reese.

And smiled.

Claudia didn't think she'd fallen asleep—she'd been only drifting—but something started her into full consciousness. She blinked, clearing her head and her vision.

Full dark had fallen; the only illumination in the room was from the lily lamp beside her…

…and a white taper candle in a simple pewter holder, burning in the window.

She sat bolt upright, looked around. At the edge of her sight she saw movement, a flash of white, in a shadowed corner of the room—but when she turned, it disappeared.

The hell?

Her heart pounding, she skirted the sofa and occasional table and a plant stand to get to the corner, where an interior wall met an outer wall, near where she'd stood to look out the window earlier.

Nothing there but paneled walls of stained fir. She reached out a hand…

And suddenly the room was filled with light.

Claudia *eeped* and spun, only to dissolve into relieved laughter when she saw Reese in the doorway, his hand at the push-button light switch.

"You startled me!" she said, her hand on her chest. If she'd thought her heart was pounding before…holy moly.

But now her heart was pounding for a different reason.

"There's a candle," he said. It would have been a non sequitur under any other circumstances.

"I fell asleep," she said as he walked towards her, which made her heart do a little kathump in between the thuds. She was glad he was back—which didn't surprise her. "I woke up and the candle was there and then I thought I saw something in this corner, but…" She lifted her shoulders in a shrug. "I got nothin'."

"Huh," he said. He cocked his head, his shaggy black hair flowing with the movement. "That's interesting."

"Why?"

"Tom and Sherry weren't ready to leave earlier, so I went outside to look at the house from a different angle. I don't have the blueprints for the house, obviously, but the measurements I took don't quite seem to add up."

"How so?" Claudia asked.

"As near as I can tell, this room ought to be wider than it is, given the placement of the windows here in the parlor and in the smoking room," he said.

Right—he was a structural engineer. He'd notice things like that. But it wasn't just about him being an engineer; he noticed details, filed them away. Like her coffee at the diner. It was part of his competence, that quiet intelligence, and she admired it.

It was her turn to cock her head. "You don't think it's just a factor of the house being added on to over the years?"

"I don't think so—both rooms are, as near as I can tell, part of the original building."

"Huh," Claudia said. "What does that mean?"

"Let find out," he said, and started tapping on the wooden panels.

"Oh, come on," she said. "It's not like we're in an episode of *Scooby-D*—wait, go back. Does that one sound different to you?"

He went back and rapped again on one of the rectangular panels. "It does—more hollow."

He felt around the panel, and Claudia could see that it was loose. Not a huge surprise in a house this old...the surprise was when he pressed against it and slid it sideways, revealing a dark hole.

Every bad horror movie raced through her head as Reese stuck his hand in the rectangular opening and felt around. A moment later he said, "I think I feel a latch."

Another moment, and a section of the wall swung inward,

just wide enough for a not-too-large person to slip through. If the parlor weren't well lit, it would be hard to see the dark opening unless you were looking for it.

She leaned in and caught the scent of tallow. Besides, that, though, the room—or passage—didn't smell musty or unused. No cobwebs, not much dust. The space was narrow and long; the light didn't extend to the other end, but she was pretty sure there'd be another secret door leading to another room.

"You know," she said, turning to Reese, "I read something that said the Underground Railroad was active in and around Heather Mountain. John Brown's Farm is nearby."

"That makes a lot of sense," he said. "So, what are we going to do? It seems to me we've solved the mystery of The White Lady."

"I think I need to talk to Mrs. Hawley," she said.

"It's Christmas Eve," he reminded her, the blue of his eyes dark and grave.

"I know," she said, glad that he cared. "I'm not going to expose her—again, it doesn't matter to me whether the ghost is real or not. But I do need to find out the truth."

"I'd like to be there when you do," he said.

"I was planning on it," she said, and took his hand. It was, she realized, only the second time they'd held hands (the gloved handshake when they'd first met didn't count). It felt natural, as if they'd been doing it for a long time—as if they fit. His fingers twined with hers.

"It doesn't mean," he said softly, "that there isn't a happy ending."

Claudia had a feeling he wasn't just talking about the ghost.

"Let's find out," she said. She wasn't just talking about the ghost, either.

This wasn't something she wanted to do, but having Reese by her side made it easier. And just seemed right.

~

Mrs. Hawley's office was a back porch that had been converted into an interior room when additions had been made to the main house. Access was through the kitchen, and the smell of roasting turkey and sautéed onions made Claudia's mouth water.

A built-in desk took up much of one wall of the long, narrow room. Unlike the rest of the lodge, which was kept in an artfully cluttered but neat Victorian style, here papers and notebooks were scattered and piled along with office supplies, a glass doorknob, and three coffee cups. On the wall were framed pictures of who Claudia assumed were Mrs. Hawley's children and grandchildren.

"Well, hello, you two," Mrs. Hawley said, closing her laptop with a snick. "What...oh dear. I can tell by your expressions something is wrong."

Claudia looked at Reese. "Not wrong, exactly," she said, and then told Mrs. Hawley that they'd found the passageway.

The older woman's shoulders slumped. "You're right," she said. "We're almost positive the passageway was a hiding place for runaway slaves. It ends in the pantry, and from there you can get down into the root cellar, which has outside access."

"And The White Lady?" Claudia had to ask.

"It's possible—probable—that my father made her up, as a way to advertise the lodge. I kept up the ruse."

"With help, I'm guessing," Reese said.

Mrs. Hawley looked down at her hands. They were strong, sturdy, and Claudia saw she still wore her wedding ring, a plain white-gold band. "Yes," she admitted. "My son's an electrical engineer; he rigged some small effects. And I hire a girl to pose as the ghost at Christmastime, although sometimes I do it, too." She stood, looked at both of them. "You're not going to tell, are you?"

"It's Christmas Eve," Reese said. "That wouldn't be in the spirit of things."

"There's no reason to expose The White Lady as a fraud," Claudia said. "It does mean we can't feature the lodge on the show, but if the legend brings in customers, keep doing what you're doing."

"Thank you," Mrs. Hawley said with heartfelt emotion.

"You know," Claudia said, struck by inspiration, "you could come up with an even better legend about the passage and the Railroad. The ghost could be year-round, lighting a candle to let the Underground Railroad know when it's safe to come. I'm sure you could find some historical accounts to back up the story—which might make you eligible for the show. I'd be willing to help you with the research."

She didn't really have the time to do that—even while she'd been working here, she'd been doing preliminary research for three other possible show topics—but she'd grown fond of the Heather Mountain Lodge in the short time she'd been here.

Back in the parlor, looking at the decorated tree, its white lights glittering, she said to Reese, "I wish I could just grab all this and...I don't know, stop time for a little while." She laughed, swirling the last dregs of her whiskey in the glass. "I wish I could just live here."

"I was thinking the same thing," Reese said, and she looked up, startled. He picked up the brochures she'd left on the sofa. "In fact, I was looking at houses, somewhere to come on my time off. Maybe you should, too."

Claudia stared at him. *Tug. Click.* It didn't just make logical sense. It made *emotional* sense. She could live anywhere, and what were wishes but things to make real, if you really wanted them?

She always trusted her instincts.

She raised her glass. "And we should make a pact to meet here every Christmas?"

He smiled, but those midnight blue eyes held a hint of seriousness. "No," he said, and before the wave of disappointment could crash over her, he added, "I wouldn't want to wait that long, would you?"

Her breath caught in her throat. She'd been half-joking, not realizing how much, until this very moment, she wanted him to say something like that.

"No, I don't think I would," she said.

Now the smile reached his eyes, made them flash in the glow of the tree's lights.

There was more here, Claudia knew, than Christmas magic. Like spring waiting under the cover of snow. That's the reason people brought in trees and decked the halls with greenery: to remind them, through the long winter darkness, that the sun would return and the earth would be abundant again. She'd half-forgotten that, missing the seasons in southern California.

There were so many questions to ask and answer, but not at this moment, she decided—it was Christmas Eve. Not a time for worries or fretting about the future. A time for rejoicing in the moment.

She didn't let Reese draw her in for a kiss—she met him halfway. Finally got to indulge the feel of his hair beneath her fingertips as their lips met and the world around them swirled like snow in a snow globe, and she thought she could stay here forever in the magic. It was only when laughter and voices echoed in the foyer that they pulled apart, but not before Reese caressed her cheek and said, "Now, tell me you'd want to wait until next Christmas to do that again."

"Not on your life," she said.

Dinner was full of laughter and talking, exactly how Claudia loved it, with everyone telling stories of their day (except all Claudia said was that she'd just missed seeing the ghost, drat it all). Afterwards, there were carols around the piano—much to her surprise, Reese played. A man of many talents; she liked that.

When they went upstairs, he stopped by her door. He took her hands in his and squeezed them gently. "Sleep tight," he said.

As earlier, she didn't stop to think, didn't know she'd made a decision until she said "Oh, don't be ridiculous," untangled her fingers from his, and reached up to draw him down for as toe-curling a kiss as she could muster.

At least, it curled *her* toes. At some point, it stopped being something she was trying to do and became something they were sharing.

When they drew apart, she asked a question with her eyes, and he answered. She took him by the hand again, and led him into her room.

It was always strange, Claudia mused, when you felt entirely different—in this case, high on the giddy, bubbling joy—and nobody else seemed to notice except the person you shared it with. And except for Brittany, who walked by them and pointed meaningfully at the mistletoe they happened to be standing under.

When they kissed, they thought they heard a low, satisfied laugh, but when they broke apart, Brittany was already in the dining room, and nobody else was near.

After breakfast, they all repaired once again to the parlor. There was a new off-white candle on the windowsill, mostly burned down. Claudia glanced at the corner and smiled.

After yesterday's snowfall, the sun had come out again, glazing the snow with a brilliance almost too bright to look at. It glinted off the icicles hanging from the eaves, and turned the snow on the trees to glittering fairy dust.

Mrs. Hawley had presents for all of them: small frames of heather pressed under glass. Matt and Holly had brought handmade bookmarks for everyone; Tom and Sherry passed out little carved bear and deer that they'd picked up at a gift shop in town; and Angela gave everyone CDs of a friend's music.

Claudia gave everyone locally made maple syrup, and Reese had had a similar idea, presenting boxes of maple candy shaped like maple leaves and pine cones, so sweet it made your teeth ache.

But Reese had another present for Claudia, which he gave her after everyone had gone off to tromp in the snow.

The box was only about six inches square, so she was unprepared for the weight of it.

She tugged off the curled blue ribbon; tore off the wrapping paper, white with blue snowflakes; opened the plain box.

"Ohhh…"

She shook the snow globe, watching the tiny white flakes swirl and dance around a winter forest scene and a building that looked much like Heather Mountain Lodge.

He must have bought it that first day, when they'd gone into town so she could do her research. That made it even more special.

"A little piece of the Adirondacks to take home to California," Reese said. "And snow to get you through the warm winter."

"It's perfect," Claudia said, her voice catching. "Thank you."

And she realized, yes, snow to get her through the winter. But not winter in LA, not ever again.

He held out his hand, helped her to her feet. "Speaking of snow," he said, "let's go outside and enjoy it. I'm thinking there's a potential snowman with our names on it."

Instead, they went for a walk in the woods.

Snow clung to the branches and covered the ground, pristine. There were no signs of her footprints or of the big white dog's paw prints from just a few nights before.

Claudia's gloved hand curled around Reese's, comfortable, strangely familiar, and ever-exciting.

"I've been thinking," Reese said.

"Hm?"

"You want to move here, I want to move here, and I think, given everything, that we might as well skip a step and look at buying one house, not two, and moving here."

"You're not just…being logical, are you?" Claudia asked, because she had to be sure, had to hear him say it. "As in, we're rarely home, so why not be roommates and share a house?"

He shook his head, slowly, as he gathered her up in his arms. "No," he said. "I'm talking about *sharing* a house, and *sharing* a future."

He kissed the tip of her nose, his lips warm against her chilled flesh, then moved in for a long, slow kiss that warmed her all over.

And that was exactly how she'd hoped he'd respond.

The sun didn't last; by the next morning, clouds had muted the sky again, heavy with potential snow. Fitting, Claudia thought, that she should leave in the weather she arrived in.

"Thank you so much," Claudia said sincerely, taking Mrs. Hawley's hands between hers. She'd already reiterated her willingness to help research the lodge's connection to the Underground Railroad. "It's beautiful here, and that's because of your hospitality and love for the lodge. From the staff, to the stories…even the dog that helped me find my way here."

Beside her, she sensed Reese suddenly going still. Mrs. Hawley cocked her head.

"Dog? What dog? I don't know what you mean."

"I've been meaning to ask you about him. A big white dog, in the woods the day I arrived. It led me here, through the snow. I was lost…" She trailed off at Mrs. Hawley's confused expression.

"I haven't got a dog," the older woman said. "I don't even know anyone around here who has a big white dog." Then she looked at Reese. "Didn't you have a big white dog when you were a boy?"

Reese's face was a blank mask. "Yes. Albus."

"That's it, Albus," Mrs. Hawley said. "A sweet dog, that one."

"Well," Claudia said, trying to recover, "if you see another big white dog in the area, thank it for me. And thank you again."

Reese didn't say anything as she shouldered her pack and followed him out to his truck. Her breath misted in the air as she climbed in, dropped the pack at her feet. He turned up the heat, but it took a few minutes for the blowing air to shift from cold to warm, and by that time they were down the driveway.

The truck bumped along the lane. Why were trucks

always louder than cars inside? She'd arrived in silence, and was leaving in sound, and while in many ways she preferred the silence, she didn't like not hearing Reese's voice.

He'd pulled in on himself, and she wasn't sure if he was angry, or didn't believe her about the dog, or if he'd done a one-eighty and decided they'd moved too fast.

Hell, what had *she* been thinking, falling in love with a guy she'd barely just met?

Trust your instincts. Somehow, she didn't feel worried.

Her instincts told her to give him time.

They arrived at the station, parked in the tiny lot, which was mostly empty except for two other cars, one of which was half-covered with snow. The station itself was small, too, just a white clapboard building with a black "witch's hat" roof, steeply pointed but still covered with snow, and an additional covered waiting area with the same type of roof.

Claudia reached for the door handle, but stopped before she opened the door. Reese had shut off the truck but made no move to open his door, and even though he was just dropping her off and didn't need to come with her, something stayed her hand. Intuition, again.

He finally spoke. "Tell me about the dog," he said, looking at the slowly fogging windshield instead of her.

So she told him about being lost, and the dog coming out of the woods, and then leading her to the lodge before bounding off behind it. "Why?" she finished.

"Like Mrs. Hawley said, when I lived here as a kid, I had a White German Shepherd. One time I was walking home and the snow was so thick I lost my sense of direction, and he found me and led me home through the woods." He finally turned and looked at her, blue eyes intent. "I've never told anyone that. Not even Mrs. Hawley."

"Well," Claudia said, feeling a curious sense of warmth, like something melting beneath her breastbone, "perhaps that means we've found the ghost after all. I believe, truly, that it was Albus who found me and led me to the lodge."

A slow smile touched Reese's lips. "I believe that, too. He had good instincts, Albus did."

"Who knows," Claudia said, "maybe he's been doing it for years."

"Or maybe he just helps people I'm supposed to meet. People who…are meant to be in my life."

Claudia's heart thumped, and she smiled, too, at that. "Then I have even more reason to be grateful." Reluctantly, she added, "My train should be here any minute now."

"Then let's go," Reese said.

She exited the truck, the cold briefly sucking the air out of her lungs. She supposed if she lived here all the time, she might complain, but right now it felt exhilarating. She heaved her pack onto her shoulders, and Reese walked with her. They were the only ones there.

The snow began drifting down, fat, languid, dancing flakes.

Once they were on the wooden platform, he turned to her and said, "I have some time off in January after I finish my current project. I could come to LA…."

Claudia felt a warm flicker in her chest, like a growing flame. "I have a better idea," she said. "I'll put in for vacation time, too, and we'll meet back here."

"Have a proper stay at the lodge?" Reese's mouth quirked in a grin.

"Snuggle under the covers and look at property listings."

"I think I can distract you away from those…."

"Challenge accepted," she said.

In the distance came the faint whistle of a train, mournful and yet expectant, inviting her to another adventure. It reminded her that she loved to travel, even if she didn't want to leave just yet.

Reese cradled her face in his hands, bent to kiss her again.

With the snow swirling around them, she felt again as if they were in their own snow globe, the world existing only for the two of them, the moment locked in time.

And she knew she had a new holiday ritual, one she'd start as of next year, in their house.

She'd leave a candle burning in the window.

She knew Reese would understand.

FLOWERS FOR MARJORY

*A*h-*choo!*"

Marjory Butler blinked in surprise as the sneeze rocked her.

"Bless you," murmured an elderly man who was examining the daffodils.

"Thank you," Marjory said, then sneezed two more times in rapid succession. She dug in her tote bag for a tissue, came up with half of a paper towel, and used that to blow her nose. She hoped she wasn't coming down with a cold.

"What'll it be this week, Miss Butler?" Jenni asked. She worked behind the counter at Bloomin' Beautiful, and they often talked about flowers when the store wasn't busy.

"Some poppies, I think, and…ah-choo!" Marjory turned away and dabbed her nose with the towel. "Sorry about that. And a bunch of gardenias. Thanks." She turned away and sneezed again.

She collected the flowers and dropped them off at her apartment, arranging them in a variety of vases before she headed back to work. She admired the bright orange of the poppies, so vibrant and alive. She wished she had a house, so she could plant a wild and beautiful garden. Here, she had to make do with window boxes and cut flowers.

Marjory felt less stuffed-up at work, and thought she might be feeling better. That is, until she went out to dinner with her boyfriend, Adam.

"Oh, look, peach roses!" she said at The Rialto, the Italian restaurant that they both loved. She buried her face in the flowers on the table and promptly collapsed into a sneezing fit.

Adam took her home before dessert, expressing his concern.

"I mud be comig dowd wid a code," she said wearily. "I'll call in sig toborrow if I sdill feel bad."

His kiss goodnight on her forehead was gentle. "I hope you feel better," he said. "Call me if you need anything."

The next morning she was still stuffed up and sneezing, but she stubbornly went to work anyway—at which point, her symptoms started to clear up.

A week later, after much back-and-forth, Marjory went to the doctor. He listened to her symptoms, took her temperature and blood pressure, then sat back, nodding.

"It sounds like you're allergic to flowers," he said.

"What!" Marjory said. "But I love flowers. I always have them around."

"Surprisingly, as we get older, we can become allergic to things we weren't allergic to before," he said. "Unfortunate but true. I can take some tests, but let's start simple. Remove all the flowers from your home and your work, and avoid gardens. If your symptoms don't clear up, then we'll try something else."

With a sigh, Marjory went out the waiting room.

"Adam! What are you doing here?"

"I was worried about you," he said, hugging her. "What did the doctor say?"

Marjory relayed the information. She felt her lower lip tremble. Adam must have noticed, because he kissed her gently on the forehead.

"It'll be okay," he said. "Why don't we take the flowers you have to the nursing home? I'm sure the people there would appreciate it."

Marjory smiled. "I'd like that," she said, thinking how kind and thoughtful he was. She was lucky to have met him, she knew. He was tall and handsome, with thick brown hair and twinkling blue eyes and a ready smile. They had been dating for two years, after they'd met at the county fair.

The nursing home was thrilled by the donation and several residents thanked Marjory and Adam as they arranged the flowers in a common room. Marjory felt her spirits lifting. At least the flowers weren't being thrown away, and someone was truly appreciating them.

She went flower-less for a week, avoiding Bloomin' Beautiful and putting no blossoms in her office or home. Her symptoms were gone by the second day. At the end of the week, she bought some freesias, but within half an hour of bringing them home, she was congested and sneezing again. With a heavy heart, she accepted that the doctor was right.

"I can prescribe some antihistamines that will help when you're outside, especially now, in spring," he said. "That's when it'll be the worst. The drugs aren't a substitute, so you should avoid flowers whenever you can."

No more bright blooms in her living room or bedroom, she thought with a sigh. No more roses to fill her office with their glorious scent. No more butterflies landing on her window boxes.

Adam bought her some silk flowers, but they weren't the same. They didn't have a scent, and the hues didn't ring true to her. She purchased a coffee-table book on famous gardens and tried to cheer herself up by looking at the pictures. But it just wasn't the same. The flowers were too small, too far away. She couldn't smell them, or touch the soft petals.

She cried when she packed up all of her pretty vases, which she had collected throughout the years. Maybe she would have a yard sale at some point, she thought, but not right away. It was too soon.

One warm summer evening, when she and Adam were walking back from The Rialto (where they'd put the carnation on another table), Adam said, "I have a surprise for you."

"Oh, really?" Marjory's heart gave a little jump. Adam had been a little secretive lately, but in a good way. He would smile at her, and when she asked what he was thinking, he'd wink and change the subject.

"Let's go to my house," he suggested. They had been spending most of their time at her small apartment, because he had been doing some work on his house. The place was in disarray, he'd said, filled with sawdust and tools.

The sun hadn't yet set, and filled the horizon with streaks of pink and peach, the glowing orange orb in the center. They held hands until they got to his house, then he opened the door and ushered her in.

They walked through the entranceway into the living room. The drapes across the sliding glass door were pulled shut. Adam walked her right up to them, then said, "Close your eyes."

Marjory obliged, listening to the sound of him pulling open the drapes and then the door.

"Take a few steps forward," he said. He put an arm around her waist and guided her over the threshold. She walked, trusting him and enjoying the feeling of him holding her.

"Now open your eyes," he said.

Marjory did, and gasped.

He had built a sunroom onto the back of the house. But although it had some windows facing out towards the back yard, it was more enclosed than a normal sunroom. Because he had then painted a garden on the walls.

A riot of flowers spilled out: her favorite roses, in yellow and peach and burgundy red; bright orange poppies; sunflowers, tall and regal; bushy stalks of lavender. It was painted realistically, so she felt as though she stood in the center of an actual garden.

"Adam!" she cried. "It's beautiful!"

"There's more," he said. He was smiling so broadly that he couldn't seem to contain his emotions. He opened the back door of the sunroom and she stepped out into the backyard.

He had replaced the white picket fence with hedges and put a fountain in the middle of the yard. Stepping stones led to it and to shady trees, under which sat comfortable benches. He'd planted a small weeping willow, and she could imagine it when it grew, majestic and full. A plot to one side, bordered by bricks, was bare. Marjory turned questioning eyes to him.

"For an herb garden, if you want to grow one," he said. "I know it's not the same as flowers, but I thought you might enjoy it. I made sure that nothing back here blooms, while still trying to make it as garden-like as possible."

"Oh, Adam," she said. Tears pricked her eyes. "It's so beautiful. But it's your house. I can't believe you went to all the trouble—"

"That reminds me," he said, his smile fading a little bit. "I can't believe I almost forgot." He led her to the fountain and she sat down. Then he drew a small box out of his pocket and got down one knee.

Marjory almost couldn't breathe. Her heart thudded and her sight grew misty.

"Marjory Louise Butler," Adam said solemnly. "I made this garden for you, in the hopes that you would be willing to share it with me, and consent to be my wife."

A diamond sparkled in the center of the rose-shaped white gold ring.

She didn't make him wait a moment longer.

"Yes," she said, and threw her arms around him and kissed him, right in the middle of their garden.

CHRISTMAS EVE AT CLAREDON HALL

Frigid rain slashed down at me from every direction. The variable gusts of lashing wind made it impossible to predict from which direction the next onslaught of water would come: into my face, or down the back of my neck, no matter how many times I pulled my collar up and close. My brimmed hat was next to useless, just becoming something else I had to clutch on to with numbed fingers, along with my medical bag.

England would not see a white Christmas tomorrow.

No souls, hardy or not, should be out on a foul night like this, I thought dourly, my boots slipping in the mud of the wooded path I could barely make out in the darkness. But as the soon-to-be-installed doctor in the town, the duty fell to me—my elderly, soon-to-be predecessor was in no shape to make the journey to Claredon Hall on a howling, stormy night like this.

I'd already heard tales of Claredon Hall and its inhabitants. In towns like this, information (gossip) is bestowed like gold from a benevolent king.

One who desires your favor.

Up ahead I could hear the crashing of Monkshead River. Even in clement weather, it was a fast-running current through dangerous outcroppings of rock. Now, swollen by rain, it sounded like an angry, howling monster.

So intent was I on not slipping and falling in the mud nor missing the crossing that I neither saw nor heard the other man approaching until he was almost upon me. I skidded to a stop as he said, his voice raised to carry over the wind and water, "Well met on this ill night, sir. I hope I did not startle you."

Willing my pounding heart to slow, I peered through the rain at him. Dark hair plastered to his head and face, a face barely visible in the gloom. I couldn't make out his clothing, although somehow, I sensed he was a soldier. Perhaps something in his bearing. Either way, he didn't look or sound familiar, so someone I hadn't encountered in town yet.

"Only so far as I didn't expect another foolhardy soul to be out in this abysmal storm," I said.

"Only foolhardy souls who fear disappointing a loved one on Christmas more than a cold dousing, I suspect," he said.

"Or foolhardy souls whose profession stops for no weather." I touched my hat with my freezing hand. "Bertram Pierce, incoming town physician."

He nodded his sodden head. "Well met, sir."

"I'm headed to Claredon Hall," I added. "I hope I haven't missed the turnoff for the bridge."

"Indeed you haven't," he said. "Claredon Hall, hm? I…"

He shook his head, but began walking with me as I started out again, for I had no desire to dilly-dally until I turned into ice and shattered.

"You're familiar with Claredon Hall?" I prompted, not pressing for information, but trying to start a conversation to take my mind away from the miserable night.

"Oh yes," he said. "Quite. What brings you there on this frightful night?"

"An illness," I said. "One of the older folks."

I didn't elaborate, for that would be skirting too close to client privilege, even though I wouldn't know what the illness was until I examined Lady Shaw.

Claredon Hall, I'd been told more than once, had fallen on hard times over the past few years. Oh, the Shaws were still a generous and caring family, and they weren't destitute, not really. But poor investments, and the war, had eaten into the family fortune. The sons had gone on to banking or law —respectable professions, although somewhat looked-down-upon ones for those of higher birth. The eldest daughter, married. The family had closed off some of the house, it had been explained to me in hushed voices, and kept only a bare staff now of butler, housekeeper, one or two maids, a groundskeeper....

With the older sons and daughter away, the household consisted of the current Lord and Lady Shaw, a daughter, and a maiden aunt—the Lady Millicent Shaw I would be attending to if I made it there unscathed.

I should have called on them earlier as a matter of propriety, but I simply hadn't had the opportunity. Then the request for a doctor's visit had reached our office.

The roar of Monkshead River was louder now, and as I squinted through the rain, I thought I saw the path to take me to the bridge.

"I believe this is the way I must go," I said. I turned toward the direction of the sound. Over the bridge, and onto Claredon Hall land, with a direct route up the lawn to the manor.

My step almost lightened at the thought of being nearly there.

A hand seized upon my arm. "Wait!"

I spun around. The other man's eyes were wide beneath his water-soaked hair, the pupils dark as the night around us.

Before I could respond, he gasped, "The bridge…the bridge is out. It always goes out when the river gets this high. You won't be able to see until it's too late."

I sagged at the thought of turning around, fighting my way back through the woods and the storm, failing at my mission.

"There's another bridge upstream," he said. "Not terribly far. It's safer."

I was trusting a stranger, but I didn't see much choice, not if I was going to have a chance of examining Miss Shaw, which was my duty and responsibility.

He was correct: it wasn't terribly far until the next bridge, which I could see was intact, higher over the water than apparently the other was.

"Cross here, head left around the lake, then up to the house," he said. "Watch your footing; it'll be slippery."

"You're not headed this way as well?" I asked. As far as I knew, there were no other homes or villages in this direction for some way. Surely the Shaws would take him in for the night.

"I have…" he hesitated "…an appointment I cannot miss."

At another time I might have pressed him further, but I had been requested by the Shaws for medical purposes, and they were my priority. Plus I needed to get inside before I caught my own death from the chill.

As much as I owed him for his suggestion of a detour that might very well have saved my life.

"My thanks to you, then," I said. "I wish you nothing but the best." I turned towards the river, but over the roar I heard him call, "One more thing, please."

And again I turned back, blinking against the deluge.

"Might I beg a boon of you?" he asked. His voice shook. "Would you deliver a letter for me, to Miss Shaw? I'm not sure…I'm not sure I will make it there tonight."

"Of course," I said. "It's the least I can do."

He pressed an envelope into my hand, and I shoved it deep into my coat pocket, as far away from the rain as I could manage.

When I looked up again, he was gone, dissolved into the driving rain and night-dark forest.

On the wide wooden bridge, I looked down at the churning, frothing water, tumbling endlessly against the rocks, and could not help but suppress a shudder.

I rang the bell of Claredon House. I couldn't see much of it in the storm, though I could tell that it was made of local pale yellow stone and had several wings spreading out from the solid front. Georgian modification, I guessed, from an earlier building.

The door opened.

The butler's uniform was a bit shiny at the cuffs, and the butler himself was an older man, receding pale hair going white at the temples. But his straight-backed, solid mien and the slightest of scowls showed he was a man who took his duties seriously indeed.

"May I help you?" he asked, as if it were a common occurrence to find a drenched man on the doorstep on Christmas Eve.

"Doctor Pierce, here at the behest of Lord Shaw," I said. "I'm here to see Miss Shaw?"

"Have I heard my name?" came a voice from within. A lilting female voice.

The butler stepped aside and ushered me in with a small gesture. I entered, resisting the urge to shake my coat collar away from my sodden neck.

Stepping inside was almost a shock, especially the relative silence when the butler closed the door again the drumming of the rain. The two-story foyer was lit and warm and quiet, its pale yellow wallpaper bringing a hint of light against the darkness outside. To my right, a grand staircase swept up, the mahogany balustrade adorned with sweetly scented pine boughs.

The speaker with the melodious voice came into view.

She had chestnut-brown hair pulled back in a popular style, although her evening dress was several years out of fashion. (I had a sister who spoke knowingly about such things; I had given up protesting that I had no interest.) She had a strong nose and kind, intelligent hazel eyes. A dimple in her left cheek—a cheek flushed from, no doubt, the fire in the parlor—flashed as she smiled and held out her hand.

"I'm Miss Larissa Shaw."

I touched my fingertips to hers, nodded my head, and said, "I am pleased to make your acquaintance. But I fear I'm not here to see you, but one Miss Millicent Shaw."

"My great-aunt. Of course. You must be Doctor Pierce."

The butler cleared his throat. It had been his duty to introduce me. She smiled at him as well, and thanked him.

"If you could find Doctor Pierce some clean clothes— something of my father's should fit him, please," she added. "Then go back to your festivities, and I'll ring you if anything is needed."

He could tell by the struggle on his face that he wanted to protest, but he said, "Thank you, your ladyship," and retreated.

"Now," she said, looking at me again. "You're drenched.

Granger will procure some of father's clothes. Come to the fire to warm yourself—you must be chilled to the bone."

She kindly didn't draw notice to my soiled trousers (I'd lost my footing on my way up the sloped, slippery lawn, scraping away the grass and landing with both knees in the mud).

I tried to demur, to insist that my patient required priority, but she would have none of it.

"Great-Aunt Millie is ill, yes, but she was down for supper a few hours ago. She can wait a few moments. If you fall ill, you'll be no use to any of your patients."

So I allowed myself to be warmed by the parlor fire while we waited for Granger to return. I met Lord and Lady Shaw, Lady Larissa's parents. He was a wide-shouldered man with a strong voice, and she was elegant and courteous. A crystal glass containing two fingers of whiskey was pressed into my hands, and I accepted it as a medicinal to assist me in warming up. My first priority was to stop shivering.

Granger showed me to a cloakroom where I changed into the dry clothing (a bit snug in some places and loose in others), after which I insisted on seeing the patient.

"Follow me," Lady Larissa said, and of course I had no option but to do so.

"Every year just before Christmas, my great-aunt insists on walking the grounds, no matter the weather," she said as we headed up the grand staircase. The scent of pine filled my nose, bringing memories of Christmases past. "As you've seen, this year has been particularly bad, and she's caught a chill."

"Why does she do this? Walk the grounds, I mean."

Lady Larissa sighed. I stopped and looked at her, and saw a sadness in her hazel eyes. "Great-Aunt Millie was engaged to a man who went to war. He swore he'd be home for

Christmas—she'd had correspondence from him confirming that he was alive and well, out of danger, and on his way."

"But he didn't arrive," I guessed.

"No. On Christmas Day, Wilifred, Earl of Spotswood, visited with the news that Great-Aunt Millie's fiancé had perished, not in the war, but by losing his step and plunging into the Monkshead River. His body had been found down-river, battered by the rocks."

"Your poor great-aunt," I said. "And the poor man, to have survived so much, only to…"

"Quite tragic," Lady Larissa agreed. "The curious thing was, he knew this land like the back of his hand, having grown up nearby. Even though there was a terrible storm that night—I suspect as wild a night as this one—one would think he would have known what to expect."

We walked along a dark-paneled corridor. There was a fine film of dust on the plate rail. The scent of pine receded, replaced by the subtle rosewater scent Lady Larissa carried.

I cleared my throat. "Other than her holiday wanderings, how is your great-aunt's health?"

"Fit as a fiddle, really. She rarely falls ill."

In an effort to be delicate, I had made my question too vague. "I mean…her mental acuity."

"Oh, goodness!" Lady Larissa laughed shortly. "Even fitter than a fiddle. She has retained her sharp wit, and she can usually beat anyone at Whist or Dictionary."

Her sudden, unfettered laugh brought warmth to my limbs where the fire had not.

We found Lady Millicent in her bed—one with walnut barley-twist posts—propped up by pillows, a lace nightcap on her head, an alcoholic nightcap on her table, and a book in her hand.

I could tell that she was a hardy soul, but Lady Millicent's cheeks were flushed like Lady Larissa's, even though the room was cooler, despite the fire crackling sweetly in the hearth. And for Lady Millicent, it was because she had a fever. Her eyes, hazel like Larissa's, were bright. But brighter than they ought to be.

Beneath her cap, her hair was iron-gray, and the wrinkles around her mouth and eyes blossomed when she smiled at me.

"You came all this way, in the storm, for me?" she asked, her voice husky but without quaver. "I am quite grateful, although I imagine there's little you can do. I'll be fine after a wee nip of whiskey and honey, and a good sleep." She had to pause between phrases to draw in air.

"I have no doubt that you will, Lady Millicent," I said. It was a gentle lie, one I had been taught at medical college. "But your nephew requested me, and here I am."

I asked her a few questions regarding coughing, breathing, and chest pain, then listened to her lungs. Through my stethoscope I heard the distinctive crackle both I'd expected and feared.

Pneumonia.

I prescribed a dose of opium in her nightcap, and in her tea in the mornings; I'd brought enough with me for several days, thankfully. I counseled that she should take a daily hot bath—twice, if she could.

There was little else I could do. Previous doctors might have suggested leeches or other methods of draining fluid from the body, but I held no stock with that nonsense.

Despite my concerns, she seemed otherwise in fine constitution, and it was as likely as not that a few days of rest and my prescriptions would bring her back to full health.

"I'll leave you to your rest," I said, and opened my bag to return my stethoscope.

Then I saw the envelope, the one the man in the woods had entrusted to me. I had transferred it from the pocket of my sodden coat (now likely hung in the laundry belowstairs to dry) to my bag when I changed.

"One more thing," I said. "I met a man on my way here who asked me to deliver a letter to you."

Her sparse eyebrows rose. "To me?"

"To Miss Millicent Shaw," I said, just as was scripted on the envelope.

The flush on her face deepened, and her blue-veined hand trembled as she took the envelope from my hand. The flap parted easily, no doubt because of the paper's dampness. She drew out several small sheets of paper. The blue ink had bled a little, even inside.

She held the letter out to Lady Larissa. "Please, dear, would you?"

Given that she had been reading a book when we entered, I wondered how bad her eyesight was…until it occurred to me later that as the tale unfolded, perhaps she had known she needed witnesses—or companions—to help her bear the revelations within.

"Of course," Lady Larissa said, smoothing out the pages with slender fingers and lifting the first to the gas lamp on the wall so she could see more clearly.

My dearest Millie,

I can call you that, because we're betrothed, and no one else has to see this letter. You are mine, and I am yours, forever and beyond, as we've always said.

"Forever and beyond," Lady Shaw repeated softly, nodding.

I promised I would be home by Christmas, as by God, I nearly was. So close. I departed the train in town to a miserable storm on Christmas Eve, but I wouldn't let a little rain and wind to keep me from my beloved girl, not when I'd promised.

I could see you, dearest Millie, standing on the lawn, your lantern held high to guide me to you. So intent was I on the sight of that lantern—and you—that I failed to noticed the gap in the bridge.

But it wasn't your fault, my Millie girl, please don't think that for a moment. No, just before I set foot on the bridge, I encountered...

"Encountered whom?" Lady Millicent demanded when Lady Larissa fell silent.

"I'm afraid the ink didn't survive the rain, Great-Aunt. Let me continue and we'll see if we can't piece it together afterwards."

"Go on, then, child."

...who said that he'd just crossed the bridge and all was well.

My dearest, you are mine and I am yours, forever and beyond. Know that I loved you in this life and still love you after. You are my light and my heart.

*Yours forever
and with much fondness,
Bertie*

Lady Millicent wordlessly held out her hand, and Lady Larissa handed back the pages. Lady Millicent pressed them to her bosom.

"Thank you. Thank you." Her eyes were bright now with brimming tears as she reached out with her other hand to grasp on of mine. "I can't tell you much this means to me. He was coming home. I knew he was coming home to me."

As a man of science, despite all the evidence—the man I met who I guessed was a soldier, the story the ladies Millicent and Larissa told—it had not occurred to me until now (and even now doubt warred with what I was hearing) that the supernatural might be involved.

Despite the room's fire, despite the dry clothes I'd been

given and the whisky that had warmed me from within, I shuddered.

"He says he encountered someone on his way here," Lady Larissa mused. "Were there any guests here that evening, Great-Aunt?"

"We don't usually entertain on Christmas Eve," Lady Millicent said. "Only family."

"Yet here I am," I said lightly.

Suddenly she sat upright, which brought on a fit of coughing. She pressed a lace-edged handkerchief to her mouth, and Lady Larissa was quick to offer her some tea when the spate had ended.

"There was someone here that evening," Lady Millicent said after sipping. "Lord Spotswood." Her mouth twisted in a moue of distaste. "He was once again trying to persuade me to accept his proposal of marriage."

"But you were engaged to Albert," Lady Larissa said.

"Oh, he knew that very well, but he felt Albert was beneath me." She shook her head. "I wouldn't have said yes to Lord Spotswood if he were the last man left in England. I once witnessed him kick one of his hunting dogs so hard, the poor thing had to be put down. He was a loathsome, vile man."

A thought occurred to me, and I asked to see the letter. When it was in my hands I held it up to the lamp, examining the spot where the ink had run and blurred.

My profession had gifted me with an unlikely talent, that of deciphering poor handwriting and cryptic notations.

"It's possible," I said slowly, "that the person your Albert encountered was Lord Spotswood."

Lady Larissa took the pages from me with a delicate, long-fingered hand, and perused the same spot. "I do believe you're right, Dr. Pierce." She raised her gaze to meet mine.

Her eyes were a dusky hazel, not quite green, not quite brown. "Does that mean Lord Spotswood...?"

Her quick mind had latched on to what I had been thinking. "That he led Albert to his demise."

Lady Millicent's lips had paled as she pressed them together. "I am sorry to say, as much as the idea is repugnant, such a vile deed would not have been outside the realm of possibility for him." She shook her head slowly. "It would explain why he had been so keen to press for my hand on Christmas Eve."

"And where is Lord Spotswood now?" I asked. Despite my exhaustion from my trek through the storm, I felt a surge of chivalry, as if it had become my duty to confront the man about his potential misdeed decades earlier.

"Passed on, and no doubt damned straight to Hell's fires," Lady Millicent said. "Killed during a hunt when his horse threw him, then stepped on him." There was a dark glint in her eye when she added, "I've always imagined that horse was expressing an opinion, shall we say."

Neither Lady Larissa nor I had a response to that.

Lady Millicent sank back against her pillows, her complexion wan. The discussion had wearied her, when she was already battling illness. Lady Larissa said she would call for the nightcap, and I retreated downstairs with her to instruct the kitchen staff on the opium dosage.

Lord and Lady Shaw of course insisted I stay the night, and given the way the storm continued to rage outside, I had no desire to demur. A plate of food—leftover roasted goose and potatoes from their evening meal—had already been prepared for me. I hadn't realized how ravenous I was, but I ate as slowly as I could, for decorum's sake.

I thought I would have trouble falling asleep, my mind awhirl with the events of the evening. Had I indeed met a man in the woods? Had he indeed given me a letter from beyond the grave? I couldn't fathom it. And yet, how could I deny it?

The rain spattered like stones against the window at random intervals thanks to the changeable wind, causing me to jump at each rattle.

But the food and whiskey and warm bed, after I'd tired myself struggling through the miserable storm, had their effect, and I had no memory of dropping into sleep.

A bright shaft of sunlight woke me the next morning, finding a gap in the long drapes and resting itself across my slumbering eyelids. I rose and drew the drapes back. The sky, clear and pale blue, pretended there had been no storm. Indeed, the entire experience felt like something from a dream.

The grounds said otherwise. Slate shingles were shattered on the flagstone below me. The long gouges of my muddy footprints marred the once-manicured lawn, and the treeline was littered with fallen branches. A storm will always pass, but it will also always leave its mark behind.

I hadn't been awoken by a footman, not did I expect the family had one to spare, but when I turned from the window, I saw that my clothing hung on a valet stand. Even my hat was pressed, the brim sharp.

In the light, I could see the shabbiness in the corners of the room: the faded upholstery on one chair, the dust that had settled on the baseboards. Indeed, the bed linens last night had held a faint musty smell, but I had been far too exhausted to care. I was still grateful for the hospitality.

I dressed swiftly, as the fire was mere coals and the room had grown chill and I was shivering, and splashed my face in a basin of water before making my way downstairs.

Following voices, I found the family was in the breakfast room, except for the elder Lady Shaw.

Lord Shaw rose as I entered, holding his white linen napkin so it didn't slip from his lap. "Dr. Pierce. We thought you might appreciate not being woken early, given the late night you'd had. Happy holidays. Goodness, that was the worst storm we've had on Christmas Eve in fifty years."

"Please, join us," Lady Shaw said, indicating the polished oak buffet along one wall.

There were kippers and toast and eggs, sliced tomatoes and grilled mushrooms, and piping hot tea. The fanciful said tea, not blood, ran through the veins of a proper Englishman. As a physician, I knew better, but I couldn't deny how a bracing brew raised one's spirits.

"Thank you," I said. "I appreciate a warm meal before I take the walk back to the village. Although the storm has passed, it looks to be a cold day. I'll check on Lady Shaw before I depart, of course."

"Surely you can stay for luncheon," the younger Lady Shaw said with a pretty smile, a dimple accentuating her cheek. Her day dress today was a muted green that warmed her eyes, and her chestnut-brown hair gleamed.

"I'm afraid not," I said, returning her smile, mine albeit apologetic. "Despite the holiday, I do have duties to attend to."

The rest might well have been expected. When I went to check on Lady Millicent, I found her cold in her bed, a faint smile upon her face and the envelope against her breast.

I assured the family I would contact the coroner as soon as I returned to the village. Lady Larissa showed me to the door, tears sparkling on her pale, pretty cheeks.

I took her hands in mind. "In the light of day," I said, keeping my voice low, "are we sure of the events of last night? The letter...the letter could have been given to me by a relative of Lord Spotswood's—perhaps Lord Spotswood had deathbed remorse?"

"According to my great-aunt, Lord Spotswood died on the…died instantly," she said. "If you're questioning your experience, or from whom the letter came, well, 'There are more things in heaven and earth, Horatio, than are dreamt of in your philosophy.'"

I blinked. "You know Shakespeare."

That unfettered laugh burst forth again, albeit tempered and a bit shaky. "My parents believed we should all receive the same education, brothers and sisters alike. I'm well-versed in the bard along with many other subjects."

My esteem of Miss Shaw grew warmly in my chest.

And yet—and yet—to to agree with her theory went against everything I had learned and embraced.

And yet—and yet—could I deny my experiences from last night?

Granger's harrumph was almost silent, but nonetheless clear. I was taking liberties. I bowed my head, slid my hands away from hers, missing the warmth of her fingers.

Lady Larissa bade me a safe journey back and invited me to visit whenever I wished.

My reply was noncommittal as I touched my hat, gathered my bag, and took my leave.

I made my way cautiously down the sloping lawn, for the ground was still sodden, the mud slick beneath the grass.

Lady Larissa was a lovely young woman, and indeed I'd found myself taken with her. Her knowledge, her strength, and yes, her beauty.

But in the bright, cold light of Christmas Day, the previous evening's events seemed distant, a fever-dream. My studies, my training, all led to the immutable fact that ghosts did not exist, that spirits did not roam the land.

I was a doctor. A man of science. I understood reason and experiments and tangible evidence.

And yet, I could not deny the encounter I had had and the unearthly results.

I would have to reconcile all this within not only my brain, but my heart.

Because I also knew this: with all my heart, I wished to find every excuse to return to Claredon Hall.

GIVING TO THE NIGHT

Maggie accepted the cup of tea from the waiter and forced a smile. It wouldn't be fair to be rude to him just because she wasn't feeling friendly. "Thank you," she said. "Happy holidays."

The ruse apparently didn't work, because instead of walking away, he said, "You don't sound like they're very happy."

She considered the plain white teacup before her, cradling her hands around it for warmth. "I'm sorry. It's just...well, this was probably the wrong time of year to tell my parents that I...don't share their religious beliefs."

"And you had a row," the waiter concluded. "Finally came out of the broom closet, eh?"

Startled, Maggie finally looked up at him, unable to suppress a sudden laugh. "I've never heard it called that before. But how did you—?"

He nodded at her necklace, and she realized how he'd figured out she was pagan. Here in Glastonbury, it didn't bother her to wear the pentagram openly, something she wasn't used to. But there were far stranger things to be seen in this New Age mecca in the southwest of England.

The waiter, now that she looked at him properly, proved to be quite attractive, with longish brown hair, blue eyes, and a friendly smile that didn't fade as he dropped into the chair opposite hers. The tea shop wasn't crowded; the lunch rush had left and the tea-time regulars hadn't arrived.

"So did you fly all the way here to get away from them?" he asked.

Maggie opened her mouth to ask how he'd known she was American, then remembered her accent (or lack of it. For some reason, British people thought Americans had the accent, not the other way around.).

"Not exactly," she said. It was so nice to have someone talk to that she didn't feel strange telling him the story. "I'm studying over here, doing graduate work. I was going to go home for the holidays, but after arguing with my parents, I didn't see the point."

She didn't know how to explain to them how she felt. How could she describe the energy that spiraled up in her and made her feel a part of everything? How could she explain the utter rightness of a dual God and Goddess? How could she demonstrate that the love and respect she felt for the Earth went beyond a simple ecological whim? They just wouldn't understand.

"Do you have a place to stay?" the waiter asked.

She smiled. The holiday spirit of giving was alive and well here. "Yes, thank you. I've rented a self-catering cottage for the month." The smile turned rueful. "It's just a little bare because I didn't bring much with me when I came over to study, and most of that I left in my dorm room. It's just me and my books and my laptop right now."

The cafe door opened, letting in a gust of chill air, the

smell of rain, and a huddle of teenage goths. Maggie's waiter stood.

"Back to work," he said. "Enjoy your tea, witchy babe."

Maggie returned to the tea shop the next day, in large part because she was a terrible cook but, she knew, also in part because she hoped to meet the friendly waiter again. To her dismay, he'd been replaced by a blond girl with bright blue eyeliner and studs in her nose and right eyebrow (and who knew where else). Maggie spent the next two days on buses exploring the Uffington White Horse, the Long Man of Wilmington, and the Cerne Abbas Giant—figures cut into the chalk hillsides in Dorset and Wiltshire—and Stonehenge and the Avebury stone circles. She returned more grounded and centered (and laden with even more books on British pagan traditions), but still depressed about her inability to get through to her parents.

So she was somewhat surprised when she returned and had her tea delivered by the charming waiter who not only remembered her, but handed her a plastic carrier bag, saying,

"I was hoping you'd come back, witchy babe. I thought these might brighten up your flat."

The bag revealed a tangle of metal and rainbow color. She gently tipped the contents out onto the Formica tabletop and sorted it.

It turned out to be a variety of silver wire ornaments shaped like pentacles and crescent moons and fiery suns and spirals, with vibrant glass beads interwoven throughout. The jewel tones glittered in the fluorescent light of the cafe as she held one up.

"They're beautiful!" Maggie cried.

The waiter suddenly seemed a little shy. "They're Yule

ornaments to hang on your tree. You do have a tree in that bare little flat of yours, don't you?"

She bit her lip. "Well, no…. I could hang them around the room, though. They'll look wonderful in the windows." She picked up another and watched it sparkle in the light. "These really are gorgeous. Where did you get them?"

He shoved his hands in his pockets, a charming display of sudden bashfulness. "I made them."

Maggie's face must have shown her astonishment, because he added, "I'm an artist. I've been selling wire sculptures in shops in town for awhile now. I'm hoping to get a commission on a bigger piece soon—the town council is putting up a sculpture up next year and one of the designs they're considering is mine."

"I'm very impressed," Maggie said. She felt a little teary-eyed at his generosity—she didn't even know his name! But before she could ask, they were again interrupted by a flurry of customers, enough that she felt she had to vacate her table to allow enough space for them. She walked by the tea shop later in the afternoon, but didn't see him inside.

The next day she went back, this time with a thank-you card and the goal of at least learning his name. Her disappointment at seeing the blond girl again turned to amazement when the young woman cheerfully greeted her, vanished into the kitchen, and returned with a small potted evergreen that she deposited in front of Maggie.

"Ian said you didn't have a Yule tree," she said by way of explanation. When Maggie tried to demur, she added, "My dad has a nursery, so I got it cheap. If you can't take it back to university with you, we're planting a sacred grove in the spring and we'll add it there if you like."

Well. Maggie hugged her new tree as she leaned into the chill evening wind. At least now she knew his name.

It continued like that over the next few days: either Ian or one of his friends—who seemed to consider Maggie a friend by default—arrived with a small offering for the holidays. There were crystals and shells and pinecones and dried flowers ("For your altar, dear," the middle-aged woman said), a corn dolly, a hand-thrown bowl, a purple silk scarf painted with the Goddess and the God. None of the people would take "no" for an answer, and when she protested to Ian, he smiled and said there was nothing he could do about it. And then he would suggest they take a walk.

It didn't feel wrong when he gently took her hand one morning as they wandered through Glastonbury, ducking into different shops each time it started to spit rain. Ian was familiar with all the shops, of course, and Maggie appreciated his patience as she examined everything inside, oohed and ahhed, and asked a million questions.

"I've read a few books, but mainly I just know that it feels right," she said of paganism. "Sometimes I'm overwhelmed by how much there is to learn."

He turned to her. "What's important," he said, "is how you feel here—" and he placed a hand on her jacket just above her breast "—and here—" and his palm rested on her stomach. He tapped her on the temple. "What you think here isn't inconsequential, but it's not the most important thing."

She felt a tingle at each place where he touched her. Not magic, she knew, but something much more personal.

On another day, they climbed Glastonbury Tor, the alleged Isle of Avalon, to watch the sun set. Someone had strewn fresh pine boughs in the tower, and they breathed in the sharp holiday scent. Ian had a heavy grey cloak and he flung it over both of them against the chill. It felt so right to lean against him, feeling the beat of his heart beneath his woolly cream cable-knit sweater, and talk quietly of magic and symbols and history as the clouds in the west bloomed orange and rose and carmine.

It was there, under the flowering sunset, that they first kissed.

Maggie felt the earth tilt beneath her, and yet she had no fear, because she knew without knowing how that she was firmly connected to the ground. The first sprinkling of stars in the sky spun above them like a spiral, no beginning and no ending.

The world seemed infinite in space and possibility, and yet, at the same time, it shrank to encompass her and Ian and their embrace.

The eve of the Solstice broke the pattern of the week's rainy weather, and diamond stars glittered in the velvet sky, joined by a thin sickle moon. With the clear weather came the inevitable bite of cold, so Maggie put on her warmest sweater, an oversized red monstrosity, and shoved a matching cap in her head. Despite the cold, she went outside to wait for Ian to arrive to take her to the Solstice celebration. It gave her time to think about what he'd said.

"This is primarily a party—a celebration," Ian had explained. "However, in the past few years we've starting doing a small…I'm not even sure if 'ritual' is the right word. It's more like a meditation. You're not expected to join in so don't feel pressured to participate if you don't want to. I just want to let you know what to expect."

"Go on," Maggie said, intrigued.

"We always build a bonfire in the backyard—"

"Oh, that's fine," Maggie said dryly. "I'm not afraid of fire."

Ian laughed. Maggie liked the unselfconscious way he let loose his amusement.

"That's a start, then," he said. "Anyway, as you know, the Solstice is the longest night of the year. So, we each pick something to give up to the night—something negative. If you want, you can decide what to put in its place, although for me that doesn't usually come until later in the year. It's a sense of opening a space up for something positive to enter."

What did she want to give up to the night? Maggie wondered again as she waited in the crisp midwinter night. What did she want to unburden herself of? She shoved her hands deep into the pockets of her jeans and stared up at the glittering stars, and delved within herself. It wasn't an easy question. It seemed far safer to flinch away from negative thoughts, negative emotions. But part of what religion was for her was personal growth and betterment. If she wasn't willing to face the negatives within herself, and if she wasn't brave enough to let them go, then she couldn't open herself up to something more beneficial.

Ian's battered Mini rolled up and he jumped out before she could reach for the door handle. "Well, hello there," he said, sounding pleased. He took her cold hands, leaned in, and softly kissed her. Each time they kissed, it sent a shock-wave through her. *Ground*, she told herself firmly. It would do no good to be crackling with extraneous energy—at least, not yet.

Anne, the blond with the piercings, was hosting the party at her house outside of Glastonbury. Ian drove them through narrow winding lanes bordered by high hedgerows, pulling over in wider areas to let other cars squeeze past, their head-lights flashing their thanks.

Maggie was surprised by how many people she knew at

the gathering: It seems all of Ian's friends who'd "adopted" her over the past two weeks were there. She gladly accepted a pint of Guinness and before she knew it, was pulled in to a conversation about Green Man images and his counterpart, the sheela-na-gig. Ian stayed at her side, often with a hand resting lightly on her waist.

She liked his touch, and the smell of whatever soap he used, and the easy but intimate way he chatted with his friends. He cared about these people.

When the pencils and slips of paper were passed out, she still hadn't decided what to give up to the night, but she'd long since resolved to participate in the ritual. She smiled and nodded at Ian's questioning glance, and he smiled back, obviously relieved that she wasn't uncomfortable. They followed everyone outside to the cleared, rock-ringed space where a bonfire cheerfully pushed back the confines of the longest, darkest night.

After a moment's stillness so everyone could focus in his or her own way, people began scribbling on their papers. Maggie glanced at Ian. He was staring intently into the fire, brow furrowed slightly. She found a little surprised. He'd done this ritual before—shouldn't it be easy for him by now? Hadn't he given up enough negative things already? Goodness, he should be perfect by now! She smiled at her own silliness, at the very presumption that he couldn't continue to better himself.

And with that thought, she realized what she needed to do.

Maggie spread out the scrap of paper on her knee, wrote a single word, and firmly folded the paper several times. She stepped toward the fire and tossed the paper in, watching it catch alight and disappear into the flames. As it turned to ashes and smoke that drifted away, she willed, so would the negative….

~

They stayed at the party awhile longer, laughing and talking and drinking mulled cider, until most folks started drifting off or preparing to bed down in Anne's living room. The drive home was in companionable silence; Maggie's hand rested lightly on Ian's knee and when he wasn't shifting, he covered her hand with his own.

They stopped in front of her flat, but neither made a move to exit the car.

"Thank you," Maggie said finally. "I had a wonderful time tonight. Goodness, that sounds so trite!" she added with a laugh. "I mean it, though. Your friends have all been so kind to me, and you..."

He squeezed her hand. "I'm glad," he said finally. His voice seemed to come from far away, as if he hadn't been sure he could speak.

"What did you give to the night?" Maggie blurted. She flushed. "I'm sorry—that's probably the pagan equivalent of asking a woman her age."

He stared ahead, and she watched his profile: the strong line of his cheekbone highlighted by the streetlight, the unfocus of his eyes.

"That's okay," he said finally. His smile filled her with a rush of relief. "I don't mind telling you. I gave up fear. I've lived here all my life, I've known these people all my life, and recently I've started realizing that to have what I want, I might have to leave."

A curious warm feeling spread through Maggie's chest. But before she could ask another question, Ian broached his.

"And what, my witchy babe, did you give to the night— but tell me only if you want to."

Maggie turned her hand so that their fingers laced together. "It took me awhile to find the right word, and what

I used may not be exact, but I know what I was trying to say, what I was feeling."

"That's the important thing," he murmured.

"Presumption," she said.

"What?"

"Presumption." Maggie took a deep breath. "Looking at something and thinking it was the only way. I was presuming that paganism was simple, and I realized that I couldn't truly learn more unless I accepted how much more there was. I assumed my parents wouldn't understand, and barely gave them the chance to listen to what I was saying before cut them off. They were upset, yes, but I didn't give them the benefit of a real conversation." She took another long breath. Fear was a good thing to give up, too. She had to take the chance that she'd interpreted his words correctly. "And I presumed that when my scholarship to study here ends in June, I'd go home."

"So what are you going to do, witchy babe?" Ian's breath warmed her cheek; he was leaning quite close to her. She could smell the bonfire smoke in his hair. Maggie turned her head to face him.

"Well," she said, "it's still early in the U.S., so I'm going to call my parents. Then, when I get back to the university, I'm going to see if there's a way to extend my studies here, or what other possibilities there might be.

"As for everything else…" and she leaned so close that her lips brushed his "…I'll just have to not presume, and see where it takes me."

Maggie tried very hard not to presume anything from their ensuing kiss.

FOLLOW YOU

It was unseasonably hot, even for summer at the Cornish seaside. The unusually clear sky was an achingly beautiful shade of blue, but the lack of clouds allowed the sun to beat down unfiltered. It was that way all over England, which was why everyone and their cousin had fled to the small coastal villages.

Cate felt the sweat trickle down her back beneath the white sleeveless tee she wore, but she welcomed the heat, because it had brought out all the tourists.

So far, she'd been able to keep the throngs of people between her and the two men following her.

Chasing her, really, but she knew she couldn't move too fast or she'd stand out. People would remember her, and she couldn't have that.

The village, like so many in Cornwall, was tucked in the U of a cove bordered by high cliffs, with the town starting near the beach with shops, then houses lining the steep, narrow streets that wound up to the fertile farmland above. Verdant green above, shocking aqua below, and between them the almost too-bright white of the buildings.

Cate was short enough that she could get lost in a crowd. She chose to ease near clumps of teens, surly and slouching, pretending they didn't enjoy the seaside anymore now that they were old. The girls wore low-cut tops that also bared a flash of belly, or just bikini tops with their little shorts. The boys wore their pants around their hips, low and baggy, pretended not to be staring at the girls, and failed to notice Cate at all.

She could never have pulled this off with Daniel. Daniel stood out in any crowd: his height, his color, his condition.

"Dammit," she muttered under her breath. It had been six months, yet still she thought of Daniel during every job.

Because she was still angry that he hadn't understood her, angry that he hadn't tried, angry that he'd left her. He'd broken her heart…but if she focused on that right now, she'd get caught.

She had to focus on the job and evade the men following her.

Everyone was surlier than they ought to be, thanks to the sticky heat and the fact that the people here were the ones who hadn't been able to afford holidays to Majorca or Corfu.

The scent of brine filled the air, mixing with the sugar-sharp taste of crystallized ginger candy Cate nibbled on to add to her pretense of being just another holiday-goer.

She didn't dare look behind her to see how close the men were. She just kept moving forward, perhaps a step faster than anyone else, sliding into gaps that the larger men—"burly" was the best way to describe them—probably wouldn't even notice.

When someone brushed against her, she didn't let it distract her. Likely she was a better pickpocket anyway, and at any rate they'd be fumbling for the wallet she didn't have in her chic tote bag.

They wouldn't be after a bubble-wrapped, priceless Etruscan vase.

She saw her destination, felt a quick surge of relief that she tamped down because she wasn't out of the woods yet. Getting cocky was a surefire way of getting caught.

Tucked down a few steps against the stone seawall, the pub looked like any other: rough, whitewashed walls, grey slate roof, chalkboard stand out front advertising the local ciders and ales.

But Cate had already scouted the Tressiwick Arms for a specific purpose.

She chanced a glance over her shoulder, didn't see her pursuers, and ducked inside.

She blinked, murmuring, "Pardon me, love, that's a dear," as she slipped between patrons, waiting for her eyes to adjust to the dimness after the painfully bright sunshine. She was carrying a British passport right now, and she blended in better when she affected a generic semi-posh London accent.

Not that anyone could really hear her, between the conversations and the music. It wasn't much cooler in here, though, thanks to the crush of bodies all trying to escape the heat with a pint or three.

Thick, dark beams crossed a dirty white ceiling, and the walls were a mahogany-colored wood hung with mirrors advertising beer companies, horse brasses, and the obligatory dart board nobody was drunk enough to attempt in the tightly packed room. On the rough-hewn posts at the ends of the bar, postcards had been stuck willy-nilly with thumbtacks.

When she was close to the back of the room, she scooped up a double handful of empty pint glasses from a table— leaving the tip because she wasn't a monster—and acted as a barmaid, backing through the swinging door that led to a short hallway to the kitchen.

She quickly set the glasses on the floor along the wall. If any staff member now spotted her, she'd say she'd been looking for the loo.

Not much farther now.

She'd done her research well ahead of time. She opened the door to a small pantry—not much more than a closet, really—pushed the brooms and mops and big plastic rolling bucket aside, then pressed on the back panel.

It took a few moments to find the exact place to trip the catch, a few precious moments she didn't let herself believe she had. Sweat still tricked down her back, pooling at the waistband of her shorts.

She heard the swinging door from the bar open, bringing a surge of noise. If the employee needed something in this closet…

But then, finally, she heard a faint *snick* and the small secret door swung open, revealing the top of a set of crudely cut stone steps leading down into utter blackness.

Cate eased her phone out of her shorts pocket, but didn't turn on the flashlight yet. Instead, she ducked and stepped down into the inky darkness. Tendrils of cooler air slithered around her ankles. She placed her tennis-shoe-clad feet carefully. To say that the steps were uneven would be an understatement, and they would become damp and slick the further she went.

Once inside, she pushed the tiny door shut behind her, then turned on the flashlight app and pointed it down the corridor.

Cornwall was riddled with nineteenth-century smuggling tunnels, leading from buildings in town down to the ocean below. They'd mostly been used for sneaking in liquor and tobacco to avoid taxation.

Cate had no idea if the pub owners even knew the tunnel existed. New ones were still being found even today.

She also had no idea how burly smugglers had gotten crates of liquor, much less themselves, through such a small opening.

If her pursuers made it this far, it would be yet another thing to slow them down.

The tunnel itself wasn't very tall, either; most people would have to hunch to get through without scraping their heads on the jagged rock ceiling.

She pulled out the hidden strap in her tote bag, changing it into a cross-body bag so her hands were free, and headed down into the darkness. The steps gave way to a sloped stone floor. Her feet scuffed against a few pebbles. Beyond that, all she could hear was her own breath. When she sniffed, the sound seemed to echo. She couldn't hear the ocean yet, but she would soon.

She'd explored the tunnel system as best she could in the short time she'd had. There were several other tunnels that branched off, no doubt leading to other pubs or possibly the nearest now-disused tin mine. But all the others had been blocked by rocks, probably when work had been done on the streets above. The tunnel from the Tressiwick Arms had been her only choice.

The tunnel curved, and she went down a few more steps. The rock showed the first signs of moistness; she was closer to the ocean.

She kept an ear out for pursuit. It was unlikely at this point—they'd have to find the pub, then find the secret door.

Lord Christopher Heath-Bagley, Marquis of wherever, couldn't contact traditional law enforcement after she'd removed the Etruscan vase from his premises, given that he'd obtained it illegally himself. So he'd sent his goons after her. They'd have to return to their employer empty-handed.

Maybe it was the lack of pursuit that made her drop her guard slightly, because when someone stepped out from one

of the side tunnels in front of her—practically on top of her
—the surprise rocked her back a step.

Her heart pounding, she dropped into a fighting stance,
weight on her back leg, ready to attack or defend as needed.
She cursed herself for being unprepared.

Then cursed again when the person, so tall he had to
bend uncomfortably in the tunnel, said, "There you are, Cat."

"It's Cate," she snapped automatically. The "dammit" was
unnecessary. He'd heard it enough times before.

Daniel. He always called her Cat, short for cat burglar,
which pissed her off to no end because it belittled her job.

She tried to force her anger to take the place of her shock,
but as she straightened and pointed the flashlight at him,
seeing him, along with hearing his voice, sent a mass of
emotions cascading through her.

He was taller than her by nearly a foot, and lean. He was
stronger than he looked, and more limber than you'd expect,
both useful assets in their line of work. His ebony skin would
have been an asset as well in the dark, except for the vitiligo.
The skin disorder meant he had patches of unpigmented
skin on his face, hands, and other places on his body (some
that only someone as intimate with him as Cate would know
about, and the reminder of that made her stomach twist)—
and those patches made him stand out, under bright light or
in darkness.

He had other ways of being stealthy, though. He'd taught
Cate many of them.

And he was beautiful. She wouldn't use that word for
many men, but for him, it fit. Not just handsome. Beautiful.

"What the hell are you doing here?" she hissed, keeping
her voice low even though she was sure she'd lost her
pursuers. It also helped keep her voice from shaking—not
from the surprise anymore, but from the longing that
speared through her.

"Waiting for you, of course." He leaned against the stone wall of the tunnel. His voice was deep, like a honeyed whiskey. She would have known it anywhere.

She'd missed it.

She had an old voicemail on one of her burner phones, a phone she couldn't seem to destroy. A few times, late at night, she'd found herself listening to it. It wasn't about anything important. It was just his voice, tethering her to the earth before she spun away.

She kind of hated herself for missing it.

Now, she let that emotion take precedence, because if she didn't, this job was going all to hell.

"Did Lord Heath-Bagley hire you?"

He raised an eyebrow. "Does it matter?"

"It does to me."

He stared at her for a long time, long enough for her to get itchy and want to get back on the move. The longer she stood there, the more chilled she felt, the sweat drying and cooling on her skin.

Finally, he seemed to make a decision. "No," he admitted. "I still have an ear to the network where this kind of information shows up. I heard someone was going after the Etruscan vase, and I figured it would be you."

"So you came, here…what? To steal it for yourself?"

He scoffed. "Of course not."

"To anonymously return it?"

"If it came to that, maybe."

That's when she understood. The crux of everything they'd fought about; the reason he'd left. She almost laughed.

"You came here to persuade *me* to return it, didn't you?" She shook her head. "Daniel, Daniel. Always lawful good." He hated being called that as much as she hated being called Cat, and she took grim pleasure from the way his lips tightened.

"If you must know," she said, "a museum in Milan hired

me, because the vase had been stolen from them twenty years ago. Lord Heath-Bagley knew full well he'd purchased hot property. It's not the only piece he owns."

Daniel shook his head. "Doesn't make sense, Cat. Why didn't the TPC handle it?"

The TPC, which stood for a long Italian phrase that translated to an equally long English phrase. Short definition: the arm of the Italian army's Carabinieri police detachment dedicated to recovering stolen Italian treasures.

Okay, not a short definition after all.

"The museum worked with them and the TPC failed to track down the vase. They gave up, and the museum came to me. I've got an ear to the same network you do, buttercup, and more friends in the business because I don't judge."

Well, she hadn't used to judge. Now, she used the sources she had, but she didn't work with them anymore, and she no longer agreed with the motto of "finders keepers." The business had stopped being about just the thrill and getting hired by the highest bidder.

Daniel had been right, not that she'd ever have the chance tell him that. Even though it was his goddamn fault.

It was the reason he'd left her. She skirted too many rules —okay, as far as his conscience was concerned, she broke too many laws.

And then, after he'd walked out, the next job hadn't been as much fun. She'd thought it was because she was mourning the breakup.

The job after that left her feeling lackluster, too, and the one after that.

She took a vacation, skied in the Alps, but the siren song of the business called her back.

That was when she'd realized the allure had changed.

She glanced at her watch. She was running out of time.

The Cornish coastline was riddled with caves, and this tunnel led to one of them.

But access to the opening depended on the tide. She'd memorized the tide table. She knew just how many scant minutes of a window she had.

A part of her didn't want to leave him, but he'd already left her, so what did it matter?

"So what now?" she asked. "Are we done? I'm not returning the vase, so you might as well let me—"

In between the spaces of her words, she heard a sound.

It was hard to gauge sound in a space like these tunnels—direction, distance—but she'd had practice. And it sounded entirely like the secret door at the top of the tunnel being opened.

She stepped close to Daniel—he smelled of sweat and brine and she wanted to lick his neck but she had to focus, dammit—and whispered, "How did you get in here?"

He'd heard the noise, too, and gestured back up the tunnel. "Through the pub. I found the same plans you did. I got here a few minutes before you did."

"Were you followed?"

"I..." He closed his eyes. "I don't know. I didn't think anyone would be watching for me."

Dammit. If her pursuers thought she and Daniel were working together, they would've waited until they were in the same place. Or they hadn't figured out the secret door until she'd come along.

"I'm going," she said. "Do whatever the hell you want."

She brushed past him and moved down the tunnel as quickly as she dared. Tripping would mean disaster. She heard Daniel's footsteps behind her, soft and quick.

Hopefully their pursuers would be clumsier in navigating the passage, which would give them a few extra seconds.

No, not *them*. *Her*. She wasn't responsible for Daniel.

But as she saw the blackness ahead turn to slate grey, and finally a paling grey, enough that she could turn off her phone and shove it in her bag, she realized she sort of was.

She also didn't know if there was a third, or even a fourth man. Two had been following her, and at least one had been staking out the Tressiwick Arms.

She didn't know if the men had guns.

Either way, she couldn't abandon Daniel to them.

But her boat didn't have enough fuel to get two people where she needed to be.

Damn him.

Damn him seven ways to Sunday, in fact. Because, she saw, as the tunnel opened up into the cave, he'd delayed her long enough that the tide was going out.

The cave mouth was only accessible during a certain period in the tidal schedule. Too high, and the mouth was covered with water; too low, and you'd have to scale part of the cliff to reach it.

She pulled another, thinner bag out of her tote, dropped the tote into it, and sealed it. Waterproofed, just in case. She tucked it into a pocket in the inflatable, motorized boat she'd stashed in the cave and started tugging the boat the short way to the mouth of the cave.

Daniel grabbed the back of the boat and pushed.

At the mouth of the cave, they paused, the boat halfway off the edge, and looked down.

A few feet. Okay, not too far, but the rocks below the surface could be dangerous, and she wasn't sure just how far down they were.

"Jump shallowly," she said, just before she heaved the boat forward. It overbalanced, tipped, fell. Without waiting to see if it landed properly, she jumped.

The water was in the mid-sixties, not dangerously cold by any stretch, but still a shock even though she'd cooled down in the tunnel. She swiped the water from her face, tasting sharp ocean brine, and with a few powerful strokes was at the boat.

A splash, and then Daniel was at the boat's edge, clambering in on the other side just after her.

She hit the motor. It fired up—no small sense of relief there—and she immediately angled the boat toward the cliff. Hugging against the curved wall of rock would make it harder for their pursuers to fire at them.

She heard a shout, a curse, another splash. She glanced back. One of the men had fallen into the water. Or maybe he'd jumped, thinking he could catch them. Either way, he had a long swim around to the village cove.

More shouting, but no gunfire, and then they were far enough around that they couldn't be seen.

Cate allowed herself a sigh of relief.

There was a small cove ahead, with one set of rickety stairs leading down. Probably the village had never had the funds to put in steps that would be safe enough for tourists. England might not be as sue-happy as the states, but nobody wanted anybody falling to their doom on their summer holiday. It really put a damper on things.

Thankfully, she knew Daniel had rock-climbing experience, if it came to that.

She eased back on the motor, then cut it, and frowned. They weren't close enough to the beach yet to land.

"Daniel," she said, "I think something's caught in the propeller. Can you check?"

Then, when he bent his tall, lean frame over the rounded side of the boat, she kicked his feet out from under him.

She'd timed it correctly. The current twisted the boat enough that she could start the motor again. "Sorry!" she shouted as she went to full power away from him, out to where the village cove met the open ocean and a larger boat awaited her.

She'd escaped.

Her heart, however, hadn't been so lucky.

Milan was having the same heat wave as Cornwall, only worse, because it was far from the coast. And it had tall, modern buildings trapping the air between them. And Cate had had to put on pants and a shirt with sleeves down to her elbows in order to meet with the museum officials.

Also, for some reason, the heavy, cloying air smelled like old Band-Aids. She wrinkled her nose. Some factory, maybe.

The museum officials had been overjoyed, and the balance of the money owed had been wired into her account (and then transferred to another account, just to be safe).

She had time to indulge in one chocolate gelato before she caught her flight. Gelato shops in Italy were a dime a dozen, but Cate knew how to find the right ones. You had to look at their banana gelato. If it was bright yellow, you went somewhere else, because they'd added coloring to it. Banana gelato should be yellowy-grey like proper banana interiors.

She was sitting at a café table by the door, in the air conditioning and out of the Band-Aid smell, so she saw him coming.

Her stomach twisted painfully, and her chocolate gelato turned sour on her tongue. What the hell was Daniel doing in Milan?

She knew the answer even as she thought it. There were no coincidences. Daniel was looking for her.

Long and lean, sleek muscles under a crisp pair of khakis and a pale blue button-down shirt. He looked like a male model posing as a casual professor.

She thought about running away. The gelateria had a back door. She'd checked.

Running away seemed foolish. For one thing, what was he going to do to her? He wouldn't hurt her, and had nothing on her to turn her in for. Plus, if she ran, he'd just find her again.

Her emotions were too conflicted for her to tell how she felt about that.

So she scooped another plastic spoonful of gelato into her mouth, not tasting it, and let him find her. Even though it pissed her off that he was ruining her last chance at gelato for a good while.

"Hello, Cate," he said as he slid onto the chair across from her, and the fact that he used her proper name almost made her drop her spoon.

"What now, Daniel?" she asked. "Are you stalking me? I don't even know what my next job is, so good luck talking me out of it."

He didn't smile, and that worried her.

"I wanted to apologize," he said.

Whatever she'd been expecting, it wasn't that.

"I followed up with the museum," he continued. "The vase really was stolen."

"And I was really returning it," she said. Anger bubbled. "Did you think I was lying?"

"I didn't know what to think," he said. He toyed with a paper napkin, folding it between his long, dark fingers. "It didn't seem like your style."

"I don't think you really took the time to understand what my style is," she said. "You wanted me to become, what, an antiques dealer? Go around to black market auctions and find missing art that way?" She made a snoring noise.

"I just didn't think..." He shook his head. "We don't have to rehash it. You know what my problem was, what we didn't agree on in the business. I just…I just wanted to ask you something."

"Go ahead." Her heart was pounding. It never pounded.

No, she'd just forgotten how he could make her heart pound.

"Is this what you're doing now? Retrieving stolen things and returning them, and not merely stealing for the highest bidder?"

She sighed. She'd always had some standards, ones that he'd never been able to see or never wanted to. She'd always only stolen things that had already been stolen—she'd stolen them from their non-rightful owners. The second part had been true before, though: she'd obtained things for the person who ponied up the most money, or when it seemed like a challenging, fun job.

And that was the part that had changed.

"I have," she said. "It's cut into my profit quite a bit, but"— she shrugged carelessly to mask her true feelings—"I decided you were right. Giving things back lets me feel righteous on top of everything else."

A grin flashed across his face, and it transformed him. Making him smile had always given her a little thrill. "You mean, you've become lawful good?"

She snorted. "Good lord, no. Chaotic neutral."

"Chaotic good."

"Maybe," she conceded.

"Cate," he said, "I screwed up, big time. I didn't think you could compromise, and I didn't think I could, either, and so I bailed. And it was a mistake."

Suddenly the air conditioning felt as suffocating as the heat baking the city streets outside. But she tried to diffuse her feelings again. "Yeah, you did."

He didn't take the bait. "I did," he said somberly. "The

question is, did I screw up so badly that I've lost any chance I had with you?"

She cocked her head. She had to ask, no matter how much the question scared her. "Are you saying you want me back because I've changed?"

"No," he said, "I'm saying I want you back because you stayed true to yourself, and that's the person I never stopped loving."

Her watch chimed, reminding her of her flight.

"I've got to get to the airport," she said. "Want to come with me?"

"Depends," he said. "Are you going to push me out of a plane?"

The laughter startled out of her, and it felt good. It had been a long time since she'd laughed.

"No, I promise," she said. "Because I don't think it'll help. You'll just keep following me."

He reached for her hands, wrapped his long fingers around them, and her heart wobbled. "This time," he said, "to the ends of the earth."

THIS IS THE WORLD CALLING

*T*ansy felt as though her eyelids were lined with sandpaper. She hadn't been able to sleep on the red-eye from LAX to Vienna—her kind wasn't good with moving metal vehicles.

Contrary to popular belief, they couldn't fly. Not even on broomsticks. Pity, that.

So she'd nibbled on candied ginger to keep her stomach from rebelling, cued up her playlist of Tibetan singing bowls, and closed her eyes. But then, all she did was fret over her research project for her Global Theory class at UC Santa Barbara.

The sky was just pinkening in the east as the town car whisked her through Vienna to the hotel. It had rained overnight, and the dark pavement glittered, wet, beneath the streetlights. She was sorry she wouldn't have time to see anything of the city; she'd heard it was beautiful.

All she'd have time for was the conclave, and any moment she could sneak away from that, she'd be studying. A Masters in International Studies waited for no one, magic or not.

As the eldest, she'd have to run the family business one day.

She caught a brief glimpse of the Wiener Riesenrad, Vienna's famed giant ferris wheel, alit even at daybreak, before the sleek black car pulled up in front of the hotel where the high houses of witchcraft were meeting for their annual conclave. Heads of houses, spouses, heirs, apprentices, not to mention servants. There would be meetings, and endless suppers, and arguments. There would be schmoozing—and that really meant strengthening alliances and reaffirming who was on your side. The high houses of witchcraft were all about politics.

After all, they practically ruled the world, not that anyone else had a clue about that.

The hotel turned out to be a modern upscale one housed in the shell of a gorgeous, ancient grey stone façade. Tansy felt mildly disappointed by that; she was too exhausted to drum up real regret.

The vaulted-ceilinged, brightly lit lobby reminded her of a casino where you could never tell what time of day or night it was. The lights, after the near-darkness of the city, were jarring and made her headache flare. The lobby was dotted with sleek white leather sofas that looked supremely uncomfortable to sit in, although Tansy was so tired, she was sure she'd be able to sleep on one anyway.

The front desk clerks—there were three, even though she was the only person in the lobby other than the bellhop who'd retrieved her meager luggage from the chauffeur—were all smiles and perkiness despite the insanely early hour.

The pretty blond who helped her spoke perfect English with a delightful accent, and whisked her through check-in. Because the conclave had booked the entire hotel, it was as simple as giving her name and receiving her key card. Tansy tried not to stumble as she wearily followed the bellhop and his silent cart to her room.

The hallway smelled of magic—rosemary and lavender and woodsmoke and earthy mushrooms, all jumbled together—and she was glad when she could close the door to her room and open a window onto the dawn and the rain-soaked streets.

The room otherwise was a blur: bed, seating area, desk, lamps, black-and-white framed prints on the wall. Tansy washed her face, brushed her teeth—the peppermint soothed the last of her nausea—and started to pull off her shirt when she remembered the Do Not Disturb sign.

With a groan, she tugged her blouse back down and staggered to the door.

She opened it at the same time as the person across the hall opened his door to set out a room service tray.

"Good morning," he said with a friendly smile as he straightened, and for a moment, in her beyond-tired state, all she could do was stare. Because woah baby, was he cute.

One heart-stopping moment later, she realized he looked vaguely familiar. Since the conclave had booked the entire hotel, it was likely she'd met him, or someone in his family, before.

Narrow face with almond-shaped, blue-grey eyes, and cheekbones that could cut glass. Silky straight black hair a shade too long for propriety. Tall, slender.

Gorgeous.

"Good night," she managed, because even though it was morning her entire focus was on sleep, and closed the door, and then cursed all the way to the bed for sounding like an idiot.

Thankfully, by the time she'd stripped and crawled between the crisp white sheets and punched one of the five floofy pillows into submission, she'd forgotten her indignity.

Because she was out faster than if she'd been hit with a lose-consciousness spell.

But not before she wondered, again, how she might know the hottie across the hall.

~

She didn't sleep nearly as long as she wanted to, or as long as her body needed. But she had to force herself onto the right time schedule, and the only way to do that was force herself out of bed five hours later for lunch with her parents.

Then it was back to her room to study until the cocktail party that evening, followed by supper. "Casual enough," her mother had said. "The conclave starts tomorrow; tonight is just schmoozing."

Ah, that political schmoozing. With no formal meetings tonight, she could leave as soon as it was polite to after supper, get a few more hours of studying in, and maybe, finally, for the first time in as long as she could remember, get a full night's sleep.

Hey, a girl could dream.

She'd told her parents that she might not even make it tonight, but she'd gotten farther ahead on her work than she'd expected. A glass of Riesling and some tasty Austrian sausage and cheese, and she'd be fortified for the rest of the night.

She dressed for the evening in a knee-length emerald green dress, sleeveless, with black lace trim along the low neckline, and her favorite mid-heeled Edwardian-inspired black shoes with their pointed toes and strap across the arch of her foot. She swept her hair back with a jeweled clip, grabbed a soft black lace shawl in case the banquet room was chilly (so many were) and a clutch purse (bigger on the inside), and was ready to go.

She was thinking of him again, the man across the hall, as she opened her door.

And there he was again, just exiting his room.

His hair was pulled back into a low, short ponytail, which somehow only served to make him hotter. But his suit, while clearly tailored to his slender form, seemed off. He didn't seem the type.

Tansy forgot all that in the warm light of his smile.

"Hello there," he said. "We meet again."

Tired as she was, she still wasn't as brain-dead as she'd been during their early-morning encounter. "Not a surprise, since we're probably headed to the same function. Tansy Glass." She reached out her hand.

At the same time, he held out his and said "Hideaki Pritchard—but everyone calls me Ki."

Ki…

It was a cliché to end all clichés, but as their hands touched, Tansy heard the name echoing in her brain, and she was assaulted by a series of almost-forgotten memories.

Memories of when she was a child, and a friend she played with during the conclaves then, a little boy she'd known as Key.

—sneaking off into the New Forest and casting a faery ring of acorns and pine cones and quartz, and watching the faeries come and dance—

—on the shores of Rhine, crafting a horn to call the Lorelei—

—racing through an Andean meadow in pursuit of something real or magical or maybe crafted from their own imaginations—

Tansy tried to drop Ki's hand, but he wouldn't let go. He was clearly having the same reaction; his pupils had dilated until his eyes appeared black.

"Tansy!" he said, and his smile, if possible, grew wider, warmer. "I can't believe it—*look* at you!"

"Look at *you*," she said.

It was true. The last time she'd seen Ki, they'd been what, thirteen? Still kids, really, awkward and acned and gangly.

No wonder she hadn't recognized him, and yet had, deep down.

Then he pulled her into a hug, and the world went away again.

They'd hugged as kids, held hands, played, just been friends.

Now, her whole body shimmered with the feel of him against her, his arms around her and hers around him. She felt the strength in his slender form, the warmth of his body beneath the slate-grey silk shirt under his open jacket.

"How have you been?" he asked once he let her go (reluctantly, she hoped). "How long has it been?"

"Ten years, I think," she said. "I stopped coming because I got too busy with school."

"Me, too," he said. "Grades became so important, and getting time off was harder."

"It's still hard," she said. "I spent hours today working on a paper. But at least grad school is more flexible where classes are concerned."

"I'm already working at the family firm," Ki said, "but once I've got a foothold, I'll go back for my PhD."

"I'm exhausted just thinking about it," she said with a laugh.

"I hear you," he said. "I was up so early this morning because I couldn't sleep—I flew in from Tokyo yesterday."

"Los Angeles," she said, doing the mental calculations. "Got you beat."

It was surprisingly easy to fall into the familiarity, even

with the new frisson of interacting as intelligent, attractive adults.

"We…should probably go," Tansy said, because they still stood in the empty hallway, which probably meant the rest of the conclave members had already started schmoozing. She'd already been running late when she left her room.

"I suppose you're right," he said, reluctance in his voice, and they started walking, their feet making no sound on the plush, deep red carpet bordered with a gold Greek key design.

Unfortunately, once they got within sight of anyone else, their conversation would have to come to an end.

The feud between the Glass and Pritchard families went back so many generations, nobody remembered exactly what started it. Long, long ago, someone from one family accused someone from the other family of screwing them over, and the other family cross-accused, and it had never been resolved. It'd only gotten worse over the centuries.

It was like the Hatfields and McCoys, only on an international business level. With magic.

The Pritchards had stopped briefly to say hello when Tansy had been having lunch with her parents. Nobody had been rude, but her parents and his parents had been about as distant and impersonal and cold as anybody could be.

She could only imagine how either set of parents would react if Tansy and Ki were caught actually being more than civil to each other.

She briefly contemplated taking the stairs while he took the elevator, but she didn't want to stop talking to him just yet. They kept chatting about what they were focusing on (for him it was finance, although by the way he said it, she suspected it hadn't been his choice, but what he'd been expected to study), and their favorite past conclave adventures, and then the elevator doors opened at the lobby and everything had changed.

In hindsight, Tansy wasn't surprised that the change had happened then. Elevators were nether spaces, pockets where, if change was going to happen, it was going to happen there. The same was true of henges, certain pools, rings of fire, passageways like passage graves and yew tree walks and labyrinths, and some courtyards.

They didn't realize something had happened until they got to the room for the cocktail party and it was empty. Actually, they didn't realize it then, either, because they assumed they'd gone to the wrong room. But all the banquet and meeting rooms were empty.

And so was the lobby. And if there could be three people behind the check-in desk at four-thirty a.m., plus at least one bellhop and a concierge, there should be even more at seven o'clock in the evening.

There were none.

"Maybe there was a fire alarm, and we missed it somehow," Ki suggested.

Tansy wasn't sure how they could have missed a fire alarm that everyone else in the entire hotel had not only heard, but responded to by leaving, but it was as good a theory as they had.

They went outside into the cool Vienna evening air. The traffic noise hit them like a slap—it wasn't particularly heavy or loud, but after the relative silence inside the empty hotel, it was startling. Restaurants were open, as well as a few shops across the street.

There were no guests spread out on the sidewalk, though, nor any kind of emergency vehicles.

As they went back inside, Tansy pulled her cell phone from her purse. That was when she realized her hands were shaking. She sat on one of the white leather sofas—it was as uncomfortable as it looked—and found her mother's contact info.

Straight to voice mail. She didn't bother to leave a message. She tried calling her father; same thing.

"My parents aren't answering either," Ki said, his eyes shadowed with concern.

Tansy finally voiced what she was fearing. "Nothing short of powerful magic could take out the entire conclave," she said. "Who could've done it who isn't here? And why weren't we affected?"

"We were late to the cocktail party," Ki noted. "Maybe we didn't get swept up in it?"

For a brief moment, Tansy wondered if his parents were behind it. She wouldn't put it past them. It was an uncharitable thought, though, and she dismissed it almost immediately. If the Pritchards wanted to take everyone out, why wouldn't she have been caught up as well? And Ki seemed truly disturbed, too.

"I can't believe nobody else was late," she said. "And why would the hotel staff have been eliminated, too?"

"Like you said, if it *was* an outside force powerful enough to do this, then who?" Ki asked.

Neither of them could come up with an answer. Tansy wasn't involved enough in the family business to really know the players in the witch community, and Ki couldn't think of anyone who'd want to take everyone else down like this.

"The irony is, I was wishing we didn't have to attend the conclave," Ki admitted. He turned on the sofa to half face her, his knee brushing hers. "I wanted it to be like old times, when the two of us would just run off."

"I'd been thinking the same thing," Tansy admitted. "On the elevator…"

Their eyes met, and she knew the thought had hit both of them simultaneously.

Ki's voice was low as he said, "I don't know about you, but I don't have that kind of power."

"I don't either," she said. "But…work with me here… maybe this isn't direct magic. At least, not in the way we're thinking."

"So what is it, then?"

"Not to poke at the elephant that's always in the room," she said, "but our parents hate each other. Why in the world did they let us play together at every conclave for years?"

He blinked. "I…I've never thought about that." His shoulders raised in a slow shrug. "We were kids."

"We never thought about it while we were playing because we were kids," she agreed. "We were off in our own little world. But when we came back, my parents never said anything—did yours?"

"No. Not a word. You'd think they…" His eyes widened, and he sat up straighter. His knee was still against Tansy's, though, and despite everything, she liked having the physical contact with him. Not just because he was here and real and tangible in a moment where many others had disappeared, but because she liked how she felt when they touched.

It was Ki, comfortable and comforting…and somehow, now, more.

"Tansy, what did you just say?" he asked. "About us being in our own little world? What if it isn't that everyone's gone away…"

"…but that we've gone away from everyone," Tansy breathed. The strands of her idea finally wove together into an obvious pattern. She shivered, and fumbled her shawl over her shoulders. Even though it was flimsy lace, it seemed to help.

"Maybe that's what we've been doing all along," he said. "Our parents didn't even know we were playing together."

"We were always back before someone wondered where

we were," she said. "The conclave has always been a safe place for kids to run off and play, but we were always back by supper, or nightfall, or whenever we might start to be missed."

"Kind of," he said. "We also went back when we were done playing. When we kind of looked up and realized we'd been gone and were hungry or whatever."

"So how do we get back now?" Tansy wondered. "Just wish for it?"

They sat quietly for a moment. Tansy imagined her parents, tried to wish herself back with them. But nothing happened, and she didn't know whether to be disappointed or relieved, and then Ki said, "Sorry, I don't think I'm ready."

Tansy felt a relieved laugh burble up from inside. "Oh, thank the gods! I was afraid I wasn't able to wish hard enough!"

He laughed, too, and she was transported back to that feeling she'd had as a little girl, romping with her friend, not a care in the world.

How long had it been since she hadn't been worried about *something*? The next test or paper or goal?

"I'm not sure it's going to be as easy as wishing, anyway," Ki said. "I think we have to go play until we're done."

"I think you're right," she said. "Because if we used to go back when we were hungry, we'd be back by now, because I'm *starving*."

He grinned, a smile both boyish and devastatingly handsome, stood, and held out his hand. "Tansy Glass, will you do me the honor of having dinner with me?"

"Ki Pritchard," she said, taking his hand and standing, "as long as there's Wiener Schnitzel, it's a date."

After a brief spate of research on their phones, they chose a restaurant within walking distance of the hotel. There was indeed Wiener Schnitzel, and Spätzle, and a variety of tasty Viennese pastries.

And there was Ki, with whom Tansy alternately felt completely comfortable with because she'd know him for years and completely awkward with because she hadn't seen him for some time and now they were adults and it was different. But yet the same. She just hoped she hid any awkwardness well.

They talked about everything, it seemed: their studies, travel, the world. Movies, books (not that she had time to read for pleasure much, which she missed), magic. They decided that what they were doing—had been doing unconsciously since they were six or seven years old—was slipping out of time using their imaginations. Slipping sideways, somehow.

"I didn't even know something like this was possible," she admitted. "Now I want to go research it. Well, tomorrow I do. But imagine the implications!"

She took a sip of her Einspaenner coffee, another Viennese specialty, savoring the flavors of strong, bitter black coffee and the sweet whipped cream. A perfect balance. She hadn't had balance in her life for a long time.

"I'm almost afraid to *imagine* anything," Ki said with a laugh. "Who knows where we might end up!"

"Good point," she said. "But right now, I like the idea that we can do whatever strikes our fancy. I think we can't go back until we're done playing."

Ki handed the waiter his credit card. "Any suggestions?"

"Yep," Tansy said. "I'm finally in Vienna, and I've always wanted to ride the Riesenrad."

～

They changed clothes as they walked down the city streets to the 2nd District and the Prater amusement park. Just a subtle sheen of magic to keep anyone else from noticing. Tansy chose jeans, knee-high brown leather boots with a low heel, and a red sweater, because it was just getting chilly. Her clutch purse became a small cross-body bag. Ki switched his dress pants to jeans as well, and they fit him well, Tansy noted. He changed the suit jacket he hadn't looked happy in anyway to a black peacoat that went well with his grey silk shirt.

He slid his hand into hers, and it felt comfortable, right. His long fingers fit well with hers, and his hand was warm.

She liked touching him.

She liked how she felt when she was touching him.

She had a brief, guilty thought about her parents—were they worried about her?—but she'd told them she might not make it tonight, and that she turned her phone off when she was studying. By now they were probably embroiled in some deep negotiations anyway.

And she had a brief, guilty thought about those lost studying hours tonight. But she felt confident that her and Ki's theory was correct, that they wouldn't get back to reality until they were good and ready.

"How did you even know about this?" Ki asked as they entered the amusement park. It was free to get in, so they just started wandering through, checking out the attractions and rides.

"My dad's an old movie buff, and got me hooked," she said. "The ferris wheel—Wiener Riesenrad—was featured in *The Third Man*. It was also the world's tallest ferris wheel until 1985. It was almost a hundred years old then."

"Well, let's go, then."

Tansy stopped, craned her neck to look up at it. "Let's save it for last," she said. "Let's be kids again first."

So they did. They went on the bumper cars and bumbled their way through the mirror maze. They played arcade games, and when Ki won a big stuffed banana, he gave it to a little kid. They rode the historic carousel and flew down the giant slide and posed for selfies with wax figures at Madame Tussauds, something Tansy never would have done in other circumstances. When they actually felt a little hungry again, they bought candy at the sweet shop.

They emphatically agreed that the bungee bounce was not on the itinerary.

"I hate things that fling you around," Tansy admitted.

"Well, how about that roller coaster, then?" Ki pointed. "It's for families."

Tansy pursed her lips, eyeing it. "A baby coaster? Okay, I'm in."

There wasn't much of a line this late at night; there were fewer and fewer families wandering the park. As they drew closer, she squinted at the sign. "Dizzy Mouse?" she translated.

"The carts are mice, see?" Ki pointed.

"Yellow-and-red striped mice."

"We've unconsciously magicked ourselves into our own private reality and you have issue with mice being unusually colored?"

"Actually," Tansy said, "I'm more concerned with the fact that the mice go shooting into a giant cat's mouth. Or to be more specific, I'm concerned about where they come out."

"I don't think we're supposed to think too hard about that," Ki said. "Too late to back out now."

He was right, because they were next in line.

The round cart consisted of a long red seat that could easily fit three adults, made of hard, molded, slick fiberglass. Tansy and Ki sat in the middle, close to each other. A bar came down across their laps.

At first, their cart followed the track normally: up a slow, short incline and then into a series of curves. A few dips and bumps that were actually kind of fun. She started giggling. And then they went around a hairpin curve and the cart started to *spin*.

Even with her feet braced, Tansy was shoved into Ki as she slid on the slippery seat. But a moment later, the spin reversed, and he was shoved into her. Then they shot into the darkness of the cat's mouth, and it was ridiculous and stomach-lurching and crazy, and all she could do was laugh.

By the time they got to the end, she almost couldn't breathe, she was laughing so hard.

"Um," Ki said. "Do you want to go on it again? There's no line."

"That's okay," she gasped. "One trip through a feline digestive system is enough for me."

She was probably bruised, but she didn't care. She couldn't remember the last time she'd laughed like that, or been with someone who made her comfortable enough to howl with laughter.

His hair had come loose from the short ponytail he'd had it caught back in. Without thinking, she smoothed the dark, silky strands back from his face.

He smiled and caught her hand, pulled it down, pressed his lips against her knuckles.

Her breath caught, now for a different reason.

For a moment, they stared at each other.

"I'm still not ready to go back," Ki said.

"Of course not," Tansy said. "We still haven't gone on the ferris wheel."

The park was nearly empty, so they had the gondola to themselves. The enclosed cart could have easily fit ten people. It had wide, tall windows all around to afford the best views, with paneled wood walls beneath, and gold curtains that had been drawn back.

With a small lurch, the wheel began to turn. The gondola rocked gently. Tansy braced herself against the window, and Ki's arm came around her back. Whether it was to help support her, support himself, or draw them slightly closer together, she didn't know. Nor did she care, because if he hadn't, she'd have done the same thing.

The cart slowly rose, and they watched the rides and games of the Prater grow smaller, and the city of Vienna spread out before them, the lights like a jumbled heap of jeweled necklaces sparkling in the dark. Below, people took photos of the famous Wiener Riesenrad.

"Remember the fireflies that last year, I think when the conclave was in Michigan?" Tansy asked. "Those flashes remind me of that."

"I do remember," Ki said. "It was at that hotel on an island. We found the fairies amongst the fireflies, and brought them bread soaked in milk so they'd dance for us."

"The last thing they did was form the words THANKS FOR THE FOOD," Tansy said with a laugh. "I'd forgotten that until now. It was magical."

She realized how ridiculous it was for a witch to say that, but that thought fled when Ki said, "It still is," and kissed her.

It was a slow, gentle kiss, brief enough that she was sorry when it ended.

"What's wrong?" he asked, and until he did, she hadn't realized what she'd been holding back.

"I'm…everything is going so well," she said. "Everything always went so well. We've always been so…comfortable together. Like we fit."

"Like we belong together?"

"Yes, and that's the problem." She blew out a frustrated breath, looked out over the now-tiny city. "If there's anything

I hate in romance novels, it's when the characters are somehow destined to be together. Where's the challenge of making sure they're right for each other? I don't believe in that kind of destiny."

"I don't either," Ki said, and she felt a weight lift off. "But you can't deny we have a connection." She started to speak, but he held up a hand. "I'm not assuming anything," he went on. "Clearly our magic is compatible, which says something. But this isn't about magic, or witchcraft or conclaves or business. This is about two people—us."

"It's an 'us' that I like so far," Tansy said.

"Me, too," he said, and his fingers gently flexed against her waist, pulling her just a tiny bit closer. "We still have a lot of catching up to do, though."

"It's not going to be easy," she said, thinking of their parents, of politics, of business empires they were expected to take over someday.

"I certainly hope not," he said, and that drew a startled laugh out of her. "Otherwise, like you said, where's the challenge?"

She leaned into him then, thinking of childhood frolics and how easy it was to lose that joy when the real world intruded. She hadn't realized until now that she wanted someone to navigate through the real world with, but also run away with. Just be with.

She didn't know the adult Ki was now, but she knew the boy from the past. She'd liked him. She had no reason to believe he hadn't grown into a man she liked, too. So far, that was true.

The ferris wheel looped down and back up again as they talked more, about everything under the sun and moon, until she realized the park was long quiet and magic had taken over the controls. The moment they wanted to leave, the wheel brought them down and stopped.

Hand-in-hand, they walked through the quiet, chill streets of Vienna to the hotel as the dawn hinted at the horizon. The lobby was empty as they entered, but Tansy knew, deep down in her bones where her magic lay, that soon, the worlds would be back together, and the staff and the conclave attendees would be everywhere.

The elevator dinged, letting them out on their floor. Perhaps the change had already happened, bringing them back, given that was where it had started. But at this hour, it was impossible to tell.

"We have a few hours before the conclave starts," she noted.

"We could get some sleep," Ki said.

"I wasn't inviting you for sleep," Tansy said.

"You know," Ki said, "maybe we could use a little magic to stretch out the time just a little longer..."

As they walked down the hallway, Tansy realized she hadn't felt so relaxed in what seemed like forever. Possibly not since the last time she'd run hand-in-hand through the fireflies and faeries with Ki.

She had a feeling they could make an amazing world together.

TAKING A CHANCE

"Mom! Mom! The babysitter's here!"

Toby's voice rang out seconds after the doorbell.

"Could you answer the door, Toby?" Carolyn called out to her ten-year-old son. "I'll be right there."

She hooked simple silver hoops in ears and slipped her feet into mid-heeled black pumps. She stood, smoothing the royal blue of her skirt, and glanced at herself in the mirror. *Blind dates*, she thought, sighing. *How do I let Helen talk me into this?* But it had been a year since her divorce from Tim, and Helen was right: It was time she got back out there.

Carolyn turned away from the mirror. She either looked okay, or she didn't. It was too late to worry about it now.

She came out of the bedroom just in time to see Toby fling the door open to welcome his usual sitter, who was balancing a pizza box in one hand and a board game in the other. Neither the sitter nor Toby saw the brown streak that raced from the kitchen.

"Look out!" Carolyn cried, but it was too late. The greyhound was out the door in a flash. She ran to the door and called, "Lancelot! Here, Lancelot!"

It almost made her grin. She'd always wanted a dog named Lancelot, but her husband had hated the moniker. She'd gotten the dog a week after he left.

But the grin faded when Lancelot didn't come back. Greyhounds loved to run....

"Is he going to be okay, Mom?" Toby asked, his brown eyes wide with worry.

"I'm sure he will be," she said. "I'll go look for him."

She found her sneakers and dialled Helen's number. Stuart was new in town; Helen had only said that she knew him from college. Carolyn didn't know his last name or his phone number. She was simply supposed to meet him at the gazebo in the town park.

In five minutes. Which wasn't going to happen.

"Helen, it's me," she said after the answering machine beep. "Lancelot's run off. I'm going to be late for my date with your friend, and I don't know how to get ahold of him. Could you let him know I need to take a rain check? Thanks." She hoped the message got there in time.

She gave the babysitter instructions on what to say if either Helen or Stuart called, grabbed Lancelot's leash, and headed out.

After three hours of driving and calling his name until she was hoarse, Carolyn found Lancelot on the road out to the mill.

He loped up to her, tongue lolling out, and shook his lanky body. His mottled coat was more grey than brown, and the cloud of dust made her sneeze. She was relieved that he hadn't broken a leg or been hit by a car; she'd dreaded the thought of having to tell Toby something was wrong.

Then she saw Lancelot's nose. A long scratch ran down the length of it, oozing blood. The wound didn't look deep, but she didn't want it to get infected.

Carolyn opened the back door of the SUV and Lancelot happily jumped in. A quick check on her phone procured the number of the emergency vet. A few minutes later, she was on her way.

"Hi, I'm Dr. Franklin," said the lab-coated, sandy-haired man as he held the door to the examining room open for them. "You must be Lancelot. Up, boy."

Lancelot obediently jumped onto the examining table. He turned around twice, his paws clicking on the metal surface, and lay down.

"Ooh, that's a nasty scratch," Dr. Franklin said, gently probing the wound. Lancelot rolled his liquid brown eyes up with a look of long-suffering patience.

Carolyn, however, was watching Dr. Franklin.

He looked to be about 35, with warm blue eyes to go with his thick sandy hair. She liked the tender way he handled Lancelot, and the way the corner of his eye crinkled when he looked up at her with a reassuring smile.

"From the looks of it, he had a tussle with a cat," he said.

"That what I suspected," Carolyn said. "He'll be all right, won't he?"

"Of course. We'll just clean this up, give him a rabies booster and get some antiseptic cream on his nose, and he'll be as good as new."

"Are you new here?" she asked. "I don't think I've seen you before."

"I am at that," he said. "Just been hired." Dr. Franklin gently swabbed Lancelot's nose, while Carolyn scratched behind the dog's floppy ears to calm him. "Is he a rescue greyhound?"

"Yes," she said. "I'm really glad I got the chance to take a dog that was so in need of a home. I can't believe they just abandon them after a few years of racing."

"They've set up a lot of adoption programs, so most of the dogs find happy homes," he said, with another quick smile that warmed her to her toes. "You're a kind woman to take one of these dogs; they can be a handful. I can see he's well-cared-for."

"Thank you," Carolyn said. "I do my best. He accidentally got out tonight, and I've been looking for him for hours. I was supposed to be out on a date..."

She trailed off, mentally kicking herself. Why was she telling about that?

He nodded, and turned to get a tube of cream from the white Formica counter behind him. "I know all about that," he said. "I was supposed to go out on a blind date tonight, but I had to come into work unexpectedly when the other vet called in sick. I couldn't even call the woman I was supposed to meet, because I don't have her number."

Carolyn stared at him. Could *this* be the Stuart with whom Helen had set her up? If so, then he probably didn't know that she'd stood him up—that they'd stood each other up.

"I don't know why I let myself get talked into it," he continued cheerfully, applying antiseptic to Lancelot's scratch. "I really hate blind dates. They're so forced and artificial; you don't know what to talk about or what to do with your hands. It's not like meeting someone by chance, and then finding out that you hit it off with them." He looked up with a rueful grin. "I'm sorry. I'm just rambling on at you, aren't I?"

"It's okay," Carolyn said. "I hate blind dates, too. They make me feel kind of desperate."

"I understand," he said, pulling off his rubber gloves with a snap. "There you go, boy. You've been a good patient." Dr. Franklin gave Lancelot a pat. To Carolyn, he added, "Just make sure he doesn't rub his nose in any dirt, and put this ointment on twice a day for a week."

Lancelot jumped off the examining table, tail wagging so hard that the back end of his body shook.

"Thank you so much, Dr. Franklin," Carolyn said. They shook hands. His grip was firm, his palm cool. The contact made her insides flutter a little, in a way she hadn't felt in a long time.

"Well," she said, finally breaking away, "I'd better be getting home. Toby—he's my son—will be glad to see Lancelot."

Carolyn was surprised when she heard the doorbell ring the next morning, as she and Toby were eating their special Saturday pancakes.

"I'll get it!" Toby said, sliding out of his chair in the kitchen. He paused. "I promise to make sure Lancelot doesn't get out."

Carolyn reached over and hugged him. "I know you will, sweetheart." She'd spent quite some time last night assuaging his fears that it was his fault that Lancelot had run away.

"Hello there. Is your mother home?"

It took Carolyn a moment to recognize the voice. She fluffed her hair and tried not to feel nervous as she walked out to the hallway.

"Dr. Franklin, what a surprise," she said.

He smiled that charming smile, and she felt that flutter again. "I wanted to see how Lancelot was doing."

"Vets don't usually make house calls," Carolyn said.

He laughed. "You caught me. It was the best excuse I could come up with." He sniffed. "Do I smell coffee?"

"Would you like a cup?" Carolyn asked, and led him back into the kitchen. She grinned. Maybe she should tell him that his blind date had turned into a chance meeting after all.

PROOF OF DEVOTION

"Reverend Michaels just called," her grandmother said as Claire came in the door. "You can't get married at St. Issieu's after all."

Plastic crinkled as the wedding dress, carefully bagged, dropped from Claire's suddenly shaking hands to land on the flagstones of the 400-year-old cottage kitchen floor. "Why not?" she asked. The wedding was tomorrow.

"The sanctuary's cursed, apparently," her grandmother answered. The electric kettle snapped off, signaling that the water was boiled. "Would you like some tea?"

St. Issieu's Church perched on a ridge in the Black Mountains, overlooking a deep vale. Tangled vines of ivy and thick holly bushes, their leaves waxy and sharp, grew between the trees that lined the steep road to the church; even in the warmest days of the Welsh summer, the ancient woods felt cool, dense, secretive. The ridge on which the church sat had mostly been cleared of trees over the century, except for the combined hawthorn and ash, which were nearly as old as the church and had some how grown entwined. Next to them was a preaching cross; legend had it that Gerald Cambrensis had given a sermon from it in the thirteenth century.

Claire loved the tiny stone church, with its old paintings peering through the whitewash, and the massive rood screen, intricately carved from a single massive piece of Irish oak into lacelike leaves and dragons. From the first time she'd seen the church, she'd wanted to get married there. She wanted to walk down that short aisle, under the breathtaking rood screen, stand in the sanctuary in a medieval-style white dress, and exchange vows with the man she loved.

Once she'd recovered from her grandmother's words—and fortified by a cup of strong tea—she'd headed straight to St. Issieu's. She'd found Reverend Michaels in his study, a low, weathered wood-and-stone building next to the church that had, centuries before, served as the priest's donkey shed. The reverend let her in, offering her a cup of tea, which she declined.

"Gran says the sanctuary is cursed," Claire said. "I don't want to believe she's sudden developed dementia, but that may be the best option."

"I'm afraid it's true," he said. "The sanctuary *is* cursed." He ran a hand through his hair, which was still thick and brown despite the recession over each temple, a product of middle age.

"I was going over my ceremony for tomorrow," he said. "I thought I'd see what the parish history said about other weddings that had been held here over the years—I thought it would be nice to talk about them, tell the story of someone else who married here. That's when I found this."

He opened the dark brown leather-bound book on the

desk before him. The old pages were yellowed and ragged-edged, with a crumbly smell that made Claire want to sneeze.

"In 1129, just after the church was built, a woman named Æthelreda came to be married here. Unfortunately, it was against her will."

"I know the story," Claire said. "It's in the little photocopied brochure you leave by the side door leave for tourists. She came into the church and begged for sanctuary, but the priest refused. Her husband-to-be came in, and she tried to run, and he cut off her head. It bounced down the hill and landed by the stream, and that's what caused the well to spring up. That's why it's called St. Æthelreda's Well."

"That's only the first part of the story, apparently," Reverend Michaels said. "I didn't write the brochure, so I never knew there was more until now. Her betrothed was a powerful man, the local king. He went down there, picked up her head, put it back on her body, and married her anyway. At that point, she cursed St. Issieu's for allowing the marriage to happen. I have no idea how she got sainted after that, by the way. At any rate, she swore that any marriage that took place in the church would end in misery, just like hers."

"And you believe that?" Claire asked, incredulous.

Father Michaels set his hand on another stack of books. "I've been through all of the church records. Every marriage blessed in this church since that time hasn't lasted out its first year."

"Coincidence," Claire said promptly.

The pastor laced his hands behind his head and tilted his chair back until it balanced on two legs, creaking.

"I don't agree," he said. "A curse is a powerful thing. It's a kind of ritual, just like reciting the Lord's Prayer or taking communion. All of these do affect people."

"My wedding is tomorrow," Claire said between gritted

teeth. "I'm supposed to be in Cardiff right now, getting a massage and a manicure. I do not need this stress in my life."

"I'm honestly sorry," he said. "I can try to find another church, and we can post a notice here to the guests. I'll still perform the ceremony. You should call Jason and run it by him, too."

"We agreed not to communicate again until the wedding," Claire said. "He went to stay with friends yesterday; I don't even know which ones. It's part of the whole not-seeing-the-bride-before-the-wedding thing."

The lines at the side of Reverend Michaels's eyes crinkled deeper. "So you *do* believe in the power of ritual."

Claire fought against the panic rising in her chest, which was causing her heart to pound. "That's different," she said. "I've got something old, something new, and all that, too. It's just wedding tradition."

"All traditions started somewhere," he pointed out. He set the chair forward with a thump. "They started as ritual, and they had important meaning. We may have lost the meaning, but the strength of them doesn't diminish."

In the dingle below, nestled in a sharp turn in the road, was the holy well. The water in it ebbed and flowed depending on the force of the stream that rushed by with a sound like steadily falling rain. The stones that provided the three walls and roof over the basin of water had probably been constructed in the last hundred years, but the well itself was older than the church. Crosses made of branches hung from the stone wall beside the well and smaller ones, fashioned from twigs, had been placed inside. But also tucked in the mossy nooks and chinks were other types of offerings: feathers and pebbles and shells; scraps of paper with wishes scribbled on them before the wisher crumpled the paper tight in their fist and fervently prayed. Scraps of rags, some brightly colored, others pale and faded, fluttered in the surrounding trees.

Jason had proposed to her here, in front of the well.

Claire felt her shoulders knotting up. Dammit! She had tried so hard to make this wedding go smoothly, unstressfully. The flowers were simple, the guest list small, the wedding party just her maid of honor and Jason's best man. Her dress was custom-made, but she'd hired the seamstress well in advance. She had her mother's garter and her gran's sapphire ring. She loved Jason and had no qualms about spending the rest of her life with him. And most of all, she wanted to get married in St. Issieu's Church.

She crouched at the entrance to the well. A slab of rock slanted down towards the small, still pool. It was markedly cooler and damper in here than just outside. Claire leaned her forehead against the stone roof and closed her eyes. The smell of earth and water filled her senses.

"How could you *do* this to me?" she muttered, unsure if she were complaining to Reverend Michaels, St. Æthelreda, or fate in general. "How could you do this to me?" she repeated, louder. Finally, she shouted it, hearing her words bounce back and past her.

The wind rose, tossing the branches above her head. For a moment it seemed as though the sound of the brook rose as well, racing and rushing.

Then, in a heartbeat, it all stopped. No wind, no birds, no rustle of small creatures in the underbrush. Even the brook sounded distant, dreamlike. Claire leaned back, looked around.

In the next heartbeat, a woman appeared. She didn't so much as arrive as simply be there, where before she hadn't been.

Claire knew without a doubt what she was. She'd heard too many stories from her gran about the fair folk. She'd never really believed until now. She couldn't explain why, but she knew.

"Ah, the cry of another desperate bride." The fey's voice glinted like sun on a prism. She was tall and slender, with long wild dark hair. She smelled like the well, of damp mossy earth and icy still water and slick cold rock.

"Not exactly," Claire said. "I *want* to get married. I love my fiancé. And I want to get married in that church." Her words sounded flat in comparison.

"Never there," the faerie said. "Æthelreda's blood was shed here, on my ground, in my water. She asked for a gift, and I granted it. She used her anger to forever prevent others from suffering the same fate as she. No marriage made in that church will last more than a year and a day."

"Why?" Claire whispered. "Why must everyone suffer for what happened to her?"

"Because she believed that no woman could be happy in wedlock."

"That's not fair!" Claire said before she realized how stupid it sounded. Of course it wasn't. Life wasn't always fair, and the fey folk certainly never were. They had their own sense of justice.

"What if…" Claire chose her words carefully, not wanting to trap herself. The faeries, she knew, would capitalize on any slip. She struggled to find the right way to convey the ideas that were only half-formed in her mind. "Is there any way I could break the curse?" she asked finally.

The fey's eyebrows quirked in amusement. "An interesting proposal," she said. "I think that could be quite amusing." She pursed her lips. "All right, then. Bring me proof of your lover's devotion to you. If you convince me, then the curse will be lifted and you may marry in the sanctuary of the church. If you fail to convince me…then you and he will never wed."

Claire's breath caught in her throat. The price was high. Not as high as losing him entirely; she'd almost feared the fey would ask for his death. In that case, the answer was easy: She wouldn't take the chance. Getting married in St. Issieu's wasn't remotely as important as Jason.

Was getting married in St. Issieu's more important than not getting married at all? Although she wanted the wedding, she supposed she could live without being married. They loved each other; they'd stay together, regardless.

"You won't kill him, or harm him if I fail?" she asked, just to be clear.

"No," the fey woman said. "I will not kill him nor harm him."

Claire considered. Getting married somewhere else wasn't as good as getting married in St. Issieu's, but they'd still be married. Not getting married at all—she could live with that.

But she was certain she could prove Jason's devotion to her. She really didn't think she could lose.

"Okay," she said. "I'll do it."

"Very well. Be at the church at midnight—no later," the faerie warned. "I will make my decision then."

She was gone, and Claire was left alone by the rushing brook and dark silent well.

Gran was out when Claire got back to the cottage in Abergavenney. She was glad about that; she didn't want to explain what she was trying to do, or be distracted.

All the way home she'd thought about what to bring to

the fey to prove Jason's devotion. But by the time she pulled up the gravel drive, she still hadn't come up with anything.

Her engagement ring seemed an obvious choice. She'd watched it glinting in the late afternoon sun as she'd driven home. But while it was beautiful, and represented their promise to marry, she decided it wasn't personal enough for what the faerie was asking.

She wandered through the cottage, which she shared with Gran, picking up objects and putting them back down again. The low ceilings with their plain wood beams and the white-washed walls made everything feel small and insubstantial compared to the woods and the fey woman, Claire included. She could still smell the fey with each breath she took, and it made her a little light-headed, as if she had less mass now.

Over the edge of her mirror hung a chintzy tiara: silver-painted plastic and pasted-on rhinestones. Jason had placed it on her head on their one-month anniversary. "You make me feel like royalty," he'd said. "So you must be a princess." She smiled fondly at the memory. He never gave her gifts that didn't require a little thought, a little care, a little love. She found a box about the right size and padded it with newspaper before setting the tiara in.

Claire scanned the room again, her eyes drifting over the books on the shelves that covered an entire wall. Remember-ing, she pulled out her complete works of Shakespeare and opened to one of the sonnets. On each of four pages was a big dried oak leaf, carefully pressed. He'd written her a poem, one that had made her cry, and inscribed it on the leaves. The words, and the care he took, certainly showed his devotion to her. She put them in a plastic baggie and added them to the box.

There had to be something else. Claire sat down on the edge of the bed and thought. What were special things that Jason had given her? What had touched her heart, had made her stomach lurch like she was on a roller coaster of happiness, had caused tears to spring to her eyes?

She remembered the time she'd had chicken pox, a horrible thing to get as an adult. It hadn't been a gift he'd given her, exactly, but he'd gone out in the middle of the night, driven all the way to Cardiff to find an all-night pharmacy to buy her the special lotion to ease the itching. Claire got up and rummaged in the bathroom, unsurprised when she found the almost-empty plastic bottle. Gran never threw anything out. She put the bottle in the box.

Three things seemed appropriate; at least, that's what faeries wanted in tales, and there might be some truth in those tales after all.

She glanced out through the lace curtains. Twilight had replaced day while she had been searching. The church was only a twenty-minute drive away, half an hour if errant sheep wandered in the hedge-bordered dirt lanes. She still had plenty of time.

On a whim, she grabbed the plastic bag containing her wedding dress and zipped it open. She didn't know how long this would take in the church, and she didn't want to be late to her own wedding. Besides, it somehow seemed appropriate.

It took her some time to get into the corseted dress, and she was sure she'd pulled a muscle in her side in the process, but she eventually succeeded. Feeling more than a little silly, she strapped her fanny pack around her waist. Wedding dresses didn't have pockets, and she didn't know if she'd need her wallet or tissues.

St. Issieu's wasn't locked. It never was, because it was a tourist attraction (albeit one that appeared in only very detailed guide books). Claire pulled up on the heavy iron latch and swung the ancient oak door inwards. Chill, almost damp air greeted her, smelling of old and new, and faith. She shut the door behind her and groped behind the original 1129 stone font, now worn almost unrecognizable, for the light switch.

Claire walked slowly up the aisle between the modern pews. It was strange doing this in her dress, alone, with night crowding at the narrow windows. Just before she passed under the rood screen, she stopped. Standing on her toes, she stretched as high as she could so she could brush her fingers along the bottom edge of it, feeling the smooth wood beneath her fingers. She'd always marveled at the screen, at the work it must have taken to make such an intricate piece. The way the leaves and vines and dragons tails intertwined, with no beginning and no end. She felt like that about herself and Jason. She didn't know anymore where she ended and he began. They fit together; they completed each other.

Squaring her shoulders, she walked forward into the sanctuary. She set her box on a small glass-topped table that held one of the earliest Bibles printed in the Welsh language. Then she sat down on the cross-stitched, padded kneeling cushion, her back against the altar, and waited.

She thought about Jason, and their time together, from meeting at the Freeport Convention concert (his friends knew some of her friends, and they all went out for drinks afterwards) to yesterday when they'd kissed goodbye and he'd headed to Cardiff until tomorrow. Their relationship had had some fits and starts at the beginning, but what rela- tionship didn't? They had disagreements, but they knew how to compromise. For both of them, the other person was more important than a situation or a thing. In all honesty, Claire couldn't think of a single time he'd been hurtful or unkind.

She unzipped her pack and glanced at her watch. Four

minutes to midnight. The nervous fluttering in her stomach intensified. She had to win. She couldn't make a mistake. She loved Jason too much for that.

The faerie arrived the same way she had before, appearing between one heartbeat and the next, bringing with her the scent of earth and water and stone.

"Well met," she said. "Have you done what I have asked?"

"Yes." Claire got up and went over to the table. She opened the box. "Jason gave me this on our one-month anniversary," she said. She wondered if it were safe to give the tiara to the faerie woman; whether she would get it back. She decided it was more important not to anger her, and handed it to her. She told him what Jason had said. "He still calls me his princess," she added.

The fey was silent, regal, otherwordly. Claire took a deep breath. Okay, next try. She pulled the leaves out of the baggie, carefully, afraid that they might crumble before she could pass them on.

She showed them to the faerie one by one so that she could read it. She wasn't sure if the fair folk could read, but the woman scanned each leaf before she took it. A small nod, but still silence.

Claire's hands shook as she picked up the plastic bottle. "He didn't care about his sleep, he didn't care about how long the drive took or how many pharmacies he had to go to," she said. "He only cared that I was comfortable. I think he would've driven to London if he'd had to. I think he would've had the chicken pox for me if he could."

Still, the faerie didn't speak. Claire could hear her own breath in the silence; the church's thick walls didn't allow for any wind, any bird, any noise to enter.

"Claire?"

She hadn't heard the door open. The new voice made her start; adrenalin buzzed in her ears as she turned.

"Jason? What are you doing here?"

She watched, amazed, as he walked up the aisle. He was wearing black pants and a dark green silk shirt, and his blonde hair was pulled back in a ponytail; he must have been out at his bachelor party.

"Gran called me in a panic because you weren't home and your wedding dress was gone. She told me what Father Michaels said about the sanctuary being cursed, and I called him and he told me how upset you were. It's okay, sweetheart. I know you love this church, but we can go somewhere else. What's important is us. In fact…no. We *should* get married here. I don't care about a curse, love. I believe in us; I believe in our future."

He passed under the rood screen into the sanctuary, and stopped when he saw the fey woman, standing to one side.

"What's going on?" he asked.

Claire hugged him and buried her face in his shoulder, breathing in the scent of his sweat, not wanting to let go. But she had to. She wasn't done yet.

"It's complicated," she said.

"I have made my decision," the faerie said.

They both looked at her.

"These things are not proof enough of his devotion to you," she said.

For a moment, Claire couldn't breathe, the weight of the woman's words crushing her lungs.

The faerie stepped forward, between them, and took Jason by the arm.

"Hold on!" Claire said, panicked as Jason's eyes glazed over. "You promised you wouldn't hurt him!"

"And I shan't," the fey said. "I swear you this; I shall never harm him while he is in my thrall. But he is mine now. You agreed that if you failed, you and he would never marry. If he is with me, that will be."

"Wait! I have more proof."

Before Claire could continue, the heavy door at the back of the church swung open again. Father Michaels stepped through, already speaking.

"I wanted to give the two of you a few minutes alone to talk before I came in," he said. "Is it okay, or should I come back—" He saw the woman and froze. From the look on his face, he knew what she was, too. He crossed himself, and Claire heard him murmur "my Lord," not as a curse, but as a blessing.

"That won't affect me, I'm afraid," the faerie said. "This was our sacred ground long before men built this church and blessed it with their holy water. In fact, we appreciate that you knew the sanctity of the spot and honored it. By the same token, I cannot hurt you. But this matter is not your concern." She made a small motion with her hand. When Father Michaels tried to pass beneath the rood screen into the sanctuary, he was stopped in his tracks.

"No one shall pass in or out of the sanctuary until this matter is settled," the fey woman said.

"And it's not settled," Claire said. "I have more proof. Look at him. Look at Jason. He came all this way because he was concerned about me—as soon as he heard I was upset. He could have assumed it was normal jitters and left me alone like we'd agreed, but he came anyway, because he was worried about me." The words rushed out; she knew she was grasping. She was terrified of losing Jason. The fey had fooled her, and it was her own damn fault. She'd been an idiot, and she wouldn't be able to live with herself if that took Jason away forever.

The fey shook her head, wild haloed hair releasing the scent of darkness. "He just as well could have come because your grandmother and the church's man wanted him to, or because they told him to." She shrugged. "No proof at all."

The sanctuary seemed to swirl and tilt; Claire was being drawn down into a whirlpool of panic and despair.

"Wait!" she shouted. "Do you want proof? Fine, then, I'll give it to you." She stepped forward. "I give you *me*. *I'm* proof of his devotion. I'm a far better person for having known him; his love has given me the support and strength to succeed, to grow, to better myself. *That's* true love, dammit! I'm proof."

When the woman didn't answer, didn't move to release Jason, Claire ripped open her fanny pack and pulled out her red Swiss Army knife. With shaking fingers she pulled the biggest blade free. From behind her, she heard Father Michaels saying something, but she couldn't make out the words, and she didn't care.

"If you won't accept that, I'll spill my own blood right here on this holy site," she said, laying the knife on her wrist. "It may take awhile to get to your well, but it will. It'll seep into the ground and make its way down there, and it'll taint the water again, just like Æthelreda's blood did! That's how much I believe in his devotion."

"Claire, no!"

Somehow, Jason wrenched his mind free from the fey's spell. He pulled himself from her grasp and lunged at Claire. She took a startled step backwards and tripped on the kneeling-cushion frame. She fell, her elbow slamming painfully against the stone floor beneath the carpet. The knife bit, bright and sharp, into her arm.

Jason dropped down next to her. He picked up the fallen knife and, looking directly at the fey, drew it across his own wrist. He took Claire's arm and pressed their wrists together, wound to wound.

"You want proof of our devotion?" he asked, his voice hoarse. "Look at us. We can't share blood except for this little bit, but I promise you, I swear to you, that we're connected.

Love is something that takes a part of you and a part of the other person and twines them together, joins them. You can take me away, but you won't have all of me. A part of me will always be with her, and I'll always have a part of her with me."

"Well spoken, you both," the faerie woman said. She looked at Claire. "You have fulfilled the requirement. I could say that he helped you, but he did so through his love for you, and you for him. That is far proof enough."

Claire held her breath until the fey's next words came:

"The curse is lifted."

Claire Thomason and Jason Burnes were married by Father Joseph Michaels in St. Issieu's Church on a fine, warm June morning. The guests couldn't understand why Claire hadn't taken better care of her dress—there was a smudge on the back, a tear halfway up to her knee, and some brownish stain on the front—or why Jason had chosen to wear casual clothes instead of a tux.

They all agreed, however, that they'd never seen two people who were more in love.

THE BEST CATCH

"Oh doctor, do you think he'll live?"

The doctor turned his attention from the patient and patted my hand.

"You're being very brave," he whispered with a reassuring smile. I noticed that his eyes were very blue, like the ocean at sunrise.

We both turned back, peering into the tank.

"He's weak—listless—and his scales are flaking off," the doctor pronounced. "I'll prescribe some medication, and I'll check back over the next few days." He started sorting through the items in his satchel. I thought it was quaint that he had the traditional black bag.

"This fish must be pretty important to you," he commented as he began writing out the prescription with firm, bold strokes.

"It's not mine. It's David's—my boyfriend's. I'm taking care of the fish while he's away." I stared around the impossibly neat apartment, decorated in cold shades of grey, with chrome and glass accents. Did I really seem the type to live here? I wondered.

"These are pretty expensive tropical fish," he added, looking back into the tank. David's pride and joy, a black South American Arowanna, floated sluggishly, barely making an attempt to flap his fins, or whatever fish do. "He must really trust you," the vet went on, probably referring to David, not the fish. "How long have you known each other?"

"Four years."

I saw him shoot a glance at my left hand, but he was polite enough not to ask my mother's favorite question: "Why aren't you engaged yet, after all this time?"

The answer was…I don't know. David had made allusions to the idea, but something held me back, and he hadn't pressed. My mother pressed, because she considered David a "good catch." But it wasn't David, or the lack of engagement, that bothered me right now.

"Stupid fish," I muttered.

I hadn't meant for the vet to hear, but his eyebrows darted to a higher altitude.

"You don't like them?"

I shrugged. "They're so…unemotional." I struggled to explain the feelings I'd never put into words before. "I like pets that are aware of your existence, and can make that obvious. Affectionate. I love cats, but they don't mix well with fish," I concluded wryly.

He nodded, a lock of brown hair slipping, unruly, onto his forehead. "I agree," he said.

I wondered if he were agreeing to a preference for emotional pets or to the fact that cats and fish didn't mix. I didn't ask, though, because I also found myself comparing his shaggy, carefree hair to David's businesslike buzz.

The vet snapped his bag closed and handed me the prescription. "Put one shake of this in when you feed them."

"How much do I owe you?"

"I'll bill your boyfriend when he gets back," he said with a sudden bright grin. He handed me his business card. "Dr. Chris," it read. I smiled at the personal touch.

The next day, I eased myself into David's apartment to discover the rare black South American Arowanna had gone belly-up in the tank. One of the other fish nudged him, but apparently decided he wasn't food…yet.

"Oh no!" I moaned, leaning my forehead against the cool glass. A vision of David's wrathful face flashed before my eyes. I reach for my purse, flipped through my wallet until I found Dr. Chris' card.

"Jefferson Veterinary Clinic," answered a perky female voice. Why did that bother me? I wondered, asking for Dr. Chris.

"He's out on call right now—is this an emergency?"

I stared at the Arowanna carcass, bobbing gently in the current caused by the filter bubbles. "No," I said morosely.

I left my name and home phone number with Ms. Perky, then scooped out the unfortunate fish. Holding one hand under the net so nothing dripped on David's plush off-white carpet, I carried the Arowanna to the bathroom and gave him an undignified flush to fishy heaven. The other fish seemed to watch me suspiciously as I tapped in their food. *Murderer*, their bulging eyes seemed to accuse. But how could it be murder when the poor fish didn't even have a name?

"I almost didn't get your message," Dr. Chris said after I lunged for the phone and nearly shrieked a greeting. "Marlene, my receptionist, went into labor an hour ago and it was mayhem here for a while until her husband showed up to drive her to the hospital. How's the fish?"

"The fish is dead," I said, "and so is my relationship, unless I can find another one. Any suggestions?"

"I'm done for the day; why don't I pick you up and we'll make the rounds?"

Glad for the moral support, I agreed, wondering what David would think if he learned I'd been fish-shopping with another man. Did that constitute betrayal? Probably, given that the other man had sea-blue eyes and a rakish cowlick, and wasn't involved with his perky receptionist.

I gave him my home address and Chris—he told me I could drop the "Dr." since this wasn't an official visit—picked me up half an hour later. The good news was that he knew every pet store in the county. The bad news was that most of the stores had no clue where to find a rare black South American Arowanna, Finally, we found ourselves in the Hillsport Shopping Coliseum's Pet-O-Rama, where, ironically, David had bought the first fish.

"We don't have one in stock," murmured the sales clerk thoughtfully, "but we can certainly order one for you. It may take some time; we don't get many requests for them because they're so expensive."

"Exactly how much is this going to cost?" I asked, trying to sound confident, like it didn't really matter.

The clerk quoted a figure higher than my weekly salary. The tanks behind the clerk's head swam alarmingly before my eyes. "Thank you," I squeaked, and escaped.

Chris found me in the Food Court with my head between my knees.

"Are you okay?" he asked solicitously, laying gentle fingers on my wrist and eyeing his watch. The professional contact caused an entirely unprofessional reaction in me.

"I thought you were a vet, not a people doctor," I managed.

"Your pulse is racing," he said, a frown creasing beneath that unruly lock of hair.

You bet it is, I thought.

"Are you sure you're okay?"

"I killed his stupid fish," I moaned.

I was waiting in David's apartment when he arrived home Sunday night.

"Welcome back," I said, feigning brightness, raising my face for a kiss.

His lips brushed the air in the vicinity of my cheek. Like his fish, David wasn't big on demonstrations of affection. He handed me his suitcase and went straight to the tank.

Silence.

"Where's the Arowanna?" he asked finally. For some reason, at that moment I realized why he'd never named the fish. They weren't pets; they were investments.

"I'm afraid it died. I'm sorry," I said.

His face wasn't as wrathful as I feared, but I still didn't like the quiet way he said, "Dead?"

"Dr. Chris said it was a common disease that black Arowannas get a lot, and there wasn't any way to avoid it. The fish had most likely contracted it before you bought it. I mean, it wasn't like anyone did anything wrong." I realized I was babbling. I expected him to ask who Dr. Chris was and why I was on such a cozy basis with him.

"Do you have any idea how much that fish cost me?" David said.

The fish. Not me. He was still asking about the fish. He

hadn't even asked how I was, and he'd been gone over a week.

Why had it taken me this long to see? I pressed his apartment key into his palm, told him I would pay for the fish if he wished, and said goodbye.

Despite everything, when the phone rang the next morning, I grabbed it thinking it was David calling to apologize—or to find out if I'd sent an obituary for the fish to the local paper. I couldn't quite identify the feeling that washed over me when I heard Chris' voice instead.

"How did your boyfriend take the news?"

"Oh, swimmingly," I said ironically. "He's no longer my boyfriend."

Pause. "I'm sorry."

"I'm not." I felt a rush of freedom as I said it. "It was my choice. I guess we mixed about as well as…as oil and water."

"Or fish and cats."

"Something like that." I smiled, flattered that Chris had remembered our earlier conversation.

I thanked him for his help when I went fish-hunting, and he asked if there was anything else I needed.

"Just to be alone for a while, I guess." But as I hung up, I wasn't sure if that was true.

I had trouble concentrating at work the next day, and came home that evening feeling unsettled. When the doorbell sounded, I didn't even think it might be David. I didn't know who it could be. I had hopes….

Chris. My heart did some sort of water ballet maneuver

as he nervously ran his hand through his hair, making his cowlick stick up endearingly.

"I realize this is rather presumptuous, but I thought maybe you didn't really want to be alone." Before I could protest and invite him in, he held out a basket. A tiny butterscotch kitten mewled at me, eyes big and green and innocent.

"I've got all the supplies for him down in the car," Chris went on. "I figured he could keep you company. But if you don't want him, I can take him back…"

"No," I said quickly. "No, he's perfect. Thank you." I looked down at the kitten. He was the sweetest thing I'd ever seen. I looked back up at Chris. Okay, the second sweetest. "Won't you come in?" I said.

"I was hoping you'd ask," he admitted. "Um, would it be inappropriate to ask if you wanted to go to dinner at a really great seafood restaurant?"

It's a good thing he was still holding the basket, because I would have dropped it while I was laughing so hard.

The best catch, I'd learned, had nothing to do with fish.

THAT SUMMER ON BLUE HERON ISLAND PREVIEW

Elizabeth Sloan's idyllic annual family summer on private Blue Heron Island gets even better with the arrival of her brother's friend Will Madigan.

But handsome, charming, funny Will—who seems as

enamored of Elizabeth as Elizabeth is of him—might just be holding on to some secrets.

Has he been to Blue Heron Island before? Does he have another, more devious reason to be there now?

When sunny days dissolve into a rain-soaked night and a child disappears, Elizabeth must decide whether to trust Will with everything…including her life.

Thrilling and romantic, *That Summer on Blue Heron Island* is the perfect summer beach read! Turn the page for a sample.

CHAPTER 1

I woke to arrhythmic jolting, every shake sending a flare of agony through my head, nauseating me. Rain sheeted against my face. I tried raise my hand to block it, but my body didn't want to respond.

A flash of lightning, followed almost immediately by a long, slow grumble of thunder that seemed to go on forever, illuminated the face above me. Will Madigan, my summer crush.

Wet black hair plastered his skull. His face was pale, his lips parted as he sucked in air. He was carrying me through the dark woods, his feet thudding on the rocky, uneven path as he jogged.

I tried to ask him to stop, to put me down—my head hurt so bad—but all that came out was a low moan.

His voice was rough with emotion. "Don't you die on me, Lizzy Sloane," he said. "Don't you dare die on me."

It's Elizabeth. *Nobody calls me Lizzy anymore,* I thought grumpily, and then everything went black again.

CHAPTER 2

For as long as I can remember—which means about seventeen years, since I'm twenty now—my family has been spending summers on Blue Heron Island in Saranac Lake, New York. I think it was my great-great-grandfather who bought the island (probably bilking some Indian tribe in the process; I'm given to believe previous generations of my family didn't amass all our wealth by the most ethical of means).

My arm of the family had been the first to arrive this summer, as usual, on the heels of the cook and housekeeper (the gardener/handyman had opened up the buildings and done the grounds work, and would come back every few days as needed).

The next day, Uncle Jeremy (who was my father's half-brother) and his wife, Delilah, showed up. They have five kids: Cortland, Braeburn (Brae), Paula, McIntosh (Mac), and Fortune, all named after apples because the family had made their money with orchards. When craft brewing started to take off, they created a line of hard ciders, which was doing amazingly well. So well, in fact, that Jeremy and Delilah must have celebrated a *lot*, because Fortune was a late-in-life baby for Delilah. At eighteen months, Fortune was more than twenty years younger than her oldest bother, Cortland, and the first four kids were clumped together in age.

Cortland and his pregnant wife were here, as well as Mac, but Brae and Paula had skipped this summer. Brae was backpacking through Europe, and Paula… Well, I don't know.

Paula and Mac were a year apart, and she and I were the same age. She'd been my closest friend and confidante in the extended family for years, but in the last year or so, she'd basically ghosted me. Stopped answering my texts. Ignoring my calls. In fact, I hadn't seen her in a about a year; Delilah and Jeremy hadn't come to the island last summer, and I'd had several migraines during this past Christmas holiday, which meant I'd missed some of the family get-togethers.

It hurt, but I'd mostly shoved it aside. I'd ask Aunt Delilah when I had the chance, but I wasn't going to let Paula, or her absence, ruin my summer on the island.

That still meant there would be a bazillion people coming and going. My two aunts on my mother's side had eight kids between them, and dad's other four siblings had…this was where I had to start counting on my fingers, because I have a *lot* of cousins. Some of them might be my oldest cousins' children. If I sat down and charted it out, I'd know how everyone was related, but who wants to spend their summer vacation doing that?

Not everybody stayed all summer. Some came only for long weekends, or for a couple weeks in the middle. My older sister had just started her first year as a law clerk, so she was going to be scarce; my younger sister and brother were still in high school, so they were here but grumpy at the lack of cell service and Internet. You wanted to make a call, you went to the main lodge or the guest house and used one of the phones there.

Anyway, this year, Mac had brought his friend Will.

I was sunbathing on the beach when they arrived, lying on a towel on the sun-warmed rock, a cooler of ice and diet Coke next to me. Extra-coverage sunglasses kept the worst of the glare away from my eyes; really bright lights could trigger my migraines, but this was my favorite place in the world, and I'd learned to adapt. I didn't have my headphones on; instead, I listened to the breeze whisper through the pines and the occasional, ethereal call of a loon echoing off the water.

Perfection.

I heard the pontoon boat well before it came around the jut of land into the cove. I stood and tugged on my khaki shorts, and met them at the dock.

They'd sent ahead the bulk of their luggage, so I helped offload duffels and laptop bags and Fortune's diaper bag, hugging each family member in turn and answering the same questions every few people (when had we arrived, who else was here, how was I doing, didn't I look good?). We were loud enough that a couple of crows startled out of the trees, cawing their annoyance at the interruption to their serenity.

Mac caught me up in one of his big bear hugs. He looked as though he'd been here all summer already, with his hair a sun-bleached blond and eyebrows to match, and smelling of sunscreen. He let me go, thumped me on the back, and said "Elizabeth, this is my friend Will. Will, this is my cousin Elizabeth."

I turned with a friendly smile, and then my tongue glued itself to the top of my mouth.

Thank you, Mac, for bringing the most gorgeous friend you could find.

Thick black hair waved to his shoulders, brushed back from a high forehead and strong brow. Dark eyelashes framed intense, denim-blue eyes. Something about him looked vaguely familiar, but if I'd known someone this gorgeous in the past, I'd remember, right? Maybe he reminded me of some actor.

He grinned, a motion that lit up his face, and I found myself obsessed with his mouth. I wanted to kiss it.

I also wanted to say something witty and profound, and stop looking like an idiot.

"Hi," I said.

Damn. Not quite the pithy response I was going for.

"Nice to meet you," he said.

"Crap, my sunglasses are still in the boat," Delilah said. "Can someone grab Fortune?"

"I've got her, Mrs. Sloane," Will said, reaching out and pulling the redheaded toddler into his arms. Fortune had been fussing, but she quieted down, stuck three fingers in her mouth, and stared around, wide-eyed.

"Warning: there are going to be a lot of Mrs. Sloanes here," I said. "You might want to start calling her Aunt Delilah."

His eyebrows went up. "As long as Mac doesn't mind me joining the family."

"You're here," I said. "You don't get invited to Blue Heron Island without passing a few tests you didn't know you were taking."

I leaned my face close into Fortune's. "But you, my wittle adorable gooshy-cheeked chipmunk, you belong right here." I booped my nose against hers, and she laughed.

Will hefted Fortune more firmly in his arms and headed up the path, behind most of the rest of the group. I slung the diaper bag over my shoulder, grabbed a soft-sided cooler, and followed.

He had a great butt in a pair of tight, faded jeans. I could follow him anywhere. It was all I could do not to fan myself. My freshman boyfriend had been nothing to write home about in the end, and I'd been too busy with school to date seriously for the past two years. The summer was definitely looking up—and it had been pretty darn good to start with. Blue Heron was my happy place.

We came out of the trees and hiked up the broad steps cut into one side of the long, sloping lawn, formed by turf and old railroad ties. We piled the luggage on the flagstone patio, and Delilah took back Fortune, and the family went in to say hi to my parents and siblings.

Will stayed behind. At first this delighted me, but then I couldn't read the expression on his face as he surveyed his surroundings.

I saw the enormous but yet somehow cozy log lodge, the vast lawn that held the ghosts of a thousand games of tag, the shushing pines that surrounded us.

I was starting to worry that he, however, was scanning for a cell tower or TV dish.

"So, what is there to do around here?" he asked finally.

"It's not so much what to *do*, but how to *be*," I said, failing to keep the irritation out of my voice. It was the problem of bringing in someone new: they sometimes didn't *get* Blue Heron.

I'd had such high hopes for Will, but he was failing my test, dang it.

"It's a place to come and relax. Aunt Shannon does needlepoint, Uncle Buster annoys the cook because he loves to bake and keeps getting in the way, and my dad works on his never-ending novel. Everybody reads—there are tons of books if you don't have a Kindle. We've got board games and volleyball and badminton and croquet and kayaking and swimming and fishing. If you're really hankering for a party, there's the big Fourth of July bash that everyone comes to. Massive picnic, G&Ts out the wazoo, and yes, fireworks." I ran out of breath, sucked in some of the clean, pure mountain air.

He held up his hands. "Woah, sorry. Didn't mean to offend. Mac had warned me that it could be kind of slow, but honestly, all that sounds great. This last semester kicked my ass; it'll be nice to just kick back for awhile." He stuck one hand out. "Truce?"

Maybe I had been a little too prickly. Yeah, I had the tiniest bit of a headache coming on. "Truce."

Oh. *Oh.* His hand was warm, his fingers long and strong, curling around mind in a firm grip that went on just a little too long for my sanity. When he let go, I almost whimpered from the loss.

"How about you give me the grand tour?" he suggested.

Hell yeah. I glanced at him. He was wearing grey T-shirt with *Cornell* in red letters, the aforementioned jeans, and brown Dockers. "You might want to put on socks," I said. "Potential poison ivy."

He gave me a long, slow look, down and then up again. I felt myself flush.

"You might want to put on *clothes,*" he said.

"Well, yeah," I retorted. "Duh."

Smooth, Elizabeth, real smooth.

I also needed to grab my towel and cooler from the beach, and knock back some pain meds before the headache became a full-blown migraine.

When I was on Blue Heron I had the least number of migraines than anywhere else. My doctor figures it's because I'm so relaxed here. But they still happen every so often, and if I catch them early enough, I'm good. This one was probably a holdover from the stress of college.

I was back in my element while I showed Will around, because I could give this tour like nobody's business. Still, I'd get caught up in showing him something, turn to look at him, remember how gorgeous he was, and feel my stomach do a flip. Kind of like how it felt when I was younger and would roll down the lawn, feeling deliciously out of control.

First I showed him the rest of the lodge, the oldest standing building on the island, which was built in the 1880s and briefly served as a tuberculosis sanatorium when that was all the rage. A mix of rustic and elegant, it's like an enormous log cabin, with a two-story open living room, ten bedrooms that all have their own sinks, and enough sleeping porches, parlors, and private nooks that even when we're here in full force, it doesn't seem full. Bookshelves and artwork vie for wall space along with a couple of sad trout trophies and one moldering deer head with a faded July 4th plastic tiara dangling from one antler. His name, as I told Will now, was Fred.

"Poor dead Fred," Will said with a chuckle.

"How did you know?" I asked. "We actually call him Fred the Dead Head. I think my grandfather is responsible for that."

"Great minds think alike, I guess," Will said.

Must be.

There was one older building, at the opposite end of the island, a great stone house on a cliff overlooking the lake, which had been destroyed by fire well before I was born. Half of it is gutted; the other half a dangerous warren of rooms with fallen beams and charred wood floors. The combination of the mostly missing roof and empty windows means the wind makes some unique and spectacularly creepy moans and wails. It's a rite of passage for the younger kids to dare each other to go inside. I don't think any of us get past what would have been the foyer before running back out screaming little high-pitched kid screams.

(On a quiet day, you could hear the shrieks of the latest

crop of kids all the way to the lodge, and we'd all chuckle and shiver in memory.)

There's also a guest house and a bunkhouse, both built in the thirties, and the gaming cabin, which is basically one big room used as a children's play space when it's raining. It has a stage at one end with a closet of clothes for dress-up, hopscotch marked out on the floor, and shelves and shelves of games.

"That's new," Will murmured.

"What?" How would Will know something was new? He hadn't said he'd been here before.

He pointed to the TV and Wii and Xbox. "The gaming consoles are clearly from a more modern era."

"Well, yeah. Brendan and Constance's kids threw a hissy fit. They don't even come here much, but they insisted."

Even the other younger kids—we called them the littles— would rather be outside on a nice day. The island was paradise. Hard-packed dirt paths meandered up and down between the trees, leading to open meadows, a pond, the cove with the outthrust of rock that was the best place for fishing.

We got back in time for supper on the patio. Aunt Shannon and Uncle Buster had arrived with their five kids, all young, and we chowed into honey-glazed ham and fresh biscuits and homemade coleslaw and corn on the cob, plus Uncle Buster had made chocolate cupcakes with white frosting, our initials written on them in purple and gold.

When we were finished, Aunt Delilah had her arms full of dishes when Fortune started to fuss.

"I'll take her," I said. I cleaned her chubby cheeks and hands with a wipe, then lifted her out of her highchair into my arms. "Hello there, you squishy noodle," I crooned as I followed Aunt Delilah and Uncle Jeremy into the house.

"Hey, so how's Paula doing?" I asked.

The plates Aunt Delilah had been carrying clattered into the sink.

"Oh goodness, she's fine," she said.

"I just haven't heard from her in ages." I shifted Fortune to my other hip. "She hasn't been answering my texts."

"She's fine," Aunt Delilah repeated. "So busy with school." Her voice seemed a little high, a little shrill, but as Paula and I and the others often joked, Aunt Delilah was so jittery, she made coffee nervous. She usually calmed down by the end of the summer. Blue Heron Island worked its magic on everyone.

"She got a great internship," Uncle Jeremy said, taking over at the sink. He turned on the water to rinse the dishes, raising his voice as he added, "Really great. We won't see her all summer."

I still didn't get why Paula had ditched me like last year's fashions, but I wasn't about to say that to her parents. Aunt Delilah held her arms out, and I transferred Fortune into her arms just as I heard Mac and Will's voices as they carried in more dishes. Distracted, I ran my hands through my hair and hoped I didn't have toddler drool on me.

WHAT BECK'NING GHOST
PREVIEW

Touch not the cat bot a glove...

The MacPherson family crest above the door gives Rachael de Young, genealogist and psychic, an unexpected chill. She doesn't know that by crossing the threshold, her life will change forever. Because the MacPhersons are a family cursed by jealousy, betrayal, and fire....

Rachael grows closer to the truth even as she grows closer to the ghost of Jordan MacPherson, who died in the tragic fire...and could very well be the person sabotaging her research. But she must trust Jordan's love in order to find the strength to face her own fears, break her one cardinal rule, and stop a madman before he can kill again.

Turn the page for a sample of *What Beck'ning Ghost*, an atmospheric gothic romance from Dayle A. Dermatis.

"WHAT BECK'NING GHOST, ALONG THE MOONLIGHT SHADE
INVITES MY STEP, AND POINTS TO YONDER GLADE?"

—Alexander Pope
"Elegy to the Memory of an Unfortunate Lady"

PROLOGUE

*D*ESPITE HER PRECAUTIONARY SWEATER, Rachael found the cellared chill taking its toll; even as she felt the sneeze building she was scrabbling in the pocket of her worn jeans for a tissue. Tucking her clipboard under her arm, she blew, dislodging an errant spiral of black hair from the ribbon at the nape of her neck. She'd tied her long mane back for convenience, but it never fully responded to her taming attempts. She poised her pen over the clipboard again.

Monsieur LaFayette was gone.

Rachael muttered a minor curse under her breath, not really angry. She was used to the curator's self-absorption when it came to "his treasures."

Part of the Musée des Arts charm was that it was housed in an historic château buried deep in France's wine country. The catacombing wine cellars that ranged beneath served as storage for most of the artifacts not presently on display, walls and floors now carefully sealed to lock out damaging moisture. Fluorescent track lighting provided an unearthly glow. Crates and boxes of assorted sizes, although stacked neatly and efficiently, made each underground room a maze in itself.

"I still should've left a trail of breadcrumbs," she said aloud, propping one ink-stained hand on her hip and leaning against a towering crate marked *Full Suit of Armour, circa 14th Century; one gauntlet dented.*

As if in response, something seemed to rattle within the crate. Rachael gasped and jumped away, imagining the side of the crate swinging open and a metal-covered arm silently dragging her in next to the missing man. Still, she moved closer and peered around it, and spied the half-hidden doorway through which Monsieur LaFayette must have gone. Resisting the urge to make a notation on the wall to help her find her way back, she ducked through the low stone opening. At five-nine, she had swiftly and painfully learned to duck when she went through old doorways.

She found the rotund curator standing before a cabinet, his head barely peeking over the open door, bald skin glinting between the carefully arranged strands of sparse hair. In the cabinet were individual drawers, each labeled in the man's precise handwriting.

"Mademoiselle is not coming down with a cold, one hopes?" he asked, not looking up. His voice reflected the concern he couldn't display while he was intent on his work.

Rachael smiled, ever amused by his formal speech. If it was the last thing she did at the Musée, she was going to get him to address her by her first name.

"I'm fine," she replied honestly. The chill really didn't bother her. Her year-long study in France—and her Master's in French History—completed, she had been ecstatic to get the plum opportunity to be apprenticed to a museum curator. She'd grown to love the small Musée. What it lacked in size, it made up for with some extraordinarily rare and unique pieces of art and artifact.

In the two months she'd been there, with another month and a half to go, she'd learned nearly every facet of directing and running a museum. She felt as if she unearthed buried treasure with every artifact they systematically categorized as they moved through the storage rooms.

Monsieur LaFayette began examining each piece of jewelry in the cabinet to ensure it was undamaged. Rachael dutifully marked them down, adding notations as to what would be done with each object: remain in storage or be put on display, and in the latter case, where it might go.

"This one would go perfectly with the green velvet evening dress," Rachael said, marveling at the intricacy of a delicate silver chain studded with glinting emeralds.

"Oui, mademoiselle—that is a lovely idea," Monsieur LaFayette said, carefully replacing the necklace in its slot. "Please write that down. We will finish here today, and tomorrow we shall begin on the top floor."

The top floor was where the more perishable objects—clothing and documents—were housed. Rachael made the note on her clipboard and returned her attention to the case of jewelry.

"Gold brooch, cross-shaped, set with 4-carat, 36-point topaz," Monsieur LaFayette knelt and read off the next label, the first on the lowest row of drawers.

"That sounds like a royal jewel," Rachael commented, as he jingled his heavy set of small keys until he found the right one.

"We believe, well..." He shrugged. "It was possibly owned by Marie Antoinette," he finished softly, and sighed.

"Possib—*really*?!" Rachael couldn't contain the excitement that leapt in her belly like a frightened hare. "What's wrong?" she asked quickly, as she saw the look on the man's ruddy face.

"We believe it was given to her by a friend just after the

Cardinal of Rohan was acquitted of wrongdoing in the Diamond Necklace Affair in Versailles in 1786...but we have no documented proof," he finished sadly. "This could be the piéce de résistance of the Musée's collection, but we will never know."

"May I see it?" Rachael asked softly.

Monsieur LaFayette sat back on his haunches and smiled up at her. "Of course, mademoiselle," he said. "The brooch is quite beautiful. It is still a treasure—no matter who owned it." He slid the drawer open and, almost devoutly, brought out the carefully wrapped pouch. Rachael took it from him with solicitous hands.

As she did, she felt a chill prickle and twitch its way up her spine, a chill not caused by her current underground location. She had seen and touched many a historic object in her studies, but this one affected her differently. Could it have belonged to Marie Antoinette?

Holding her breath, she let the brooch slip from the velvet bag and cradled it in her palm. The curator was right: it *was* beautiful.

It was shaped like a cross, one long piece bisected by a shorter piece, each end flaring out into three scallops. Smaller pieces overlapped, ended in points halfway up the longer pieces. An oval band looped under all four ends, connecting them. Delicate carvings covered each piece's gold surface. The gold and topaz glimmered in the fitful fluorescent light. Rachael reverently traced a fingertip over the design. Around her, the room began to shimmer, fade at the edges.

The woman sat awkwardly in the ornate chair, her swollen belly preventing her from pulling herself close to the small writing table. The room was hot and cloying, the heat from the fireplace making Rachael's face flush. The scent of flowery potpourri was thick, almost overwhelming.

Years of study made Rachael automatically identify the woman's garments as eighteenth-century French court garb. Awed, she realized she recognized the woman from numerous portraits. Even without that, the flowery signature —"Marie Antonia"—gave no question as to the women's identity.

"June 1, 1786," she had written. "Yolande: Come and weep with me, come and console your friend. The judgment that has just been pronounced is an atrocious insult. I am bathed in tears of grief and despair." On the envelope, she carefully printed "Comtesse de Polignac." She stretched uncomfortably across the desk for the sealing wax.

Rachael fought off dizziness.

The scene changed. The woman, her figure now slim, sat very still, holding a small baby on her lap. The brooch clung to the fabric at her throat.

"T'was a gift to cheer me," she said to the painter, who had commented on the pin's beauty. Her lips thinned at the memory of why she had needed to be cheered. She forced a smile. "And to welcome Sophie Hélène Beatrice," she added, juggling the baby, who gurgled appreciatively.

Rachael shuddered, and instinctively closed her hand over the ornate pin. The images intensified.

Now the woman was gaunt, dressed in plain black, no jewels. She tried to remain regal, but her pale blue eyes revealed her fear as she was led to the guillotine. Blood red hazed the view.

Rachael pressed her hand against her mouth, muffling her own screams....

"Mademoiselle? Are you unwell? Mademoiselle de Young? *Rachael!*"

Shaking her head, Rachael pulled herself away from the images, half-reluctant to detach herself from the seductive vision. She clutched the gold-and-topaz brooch in her fist, feeling a desperate need to protect it, hide it. Monsieur

LaFayette gently pried her fingers apart and replaced the jeweled pin in its case.

"Mademoiselle?"

"I—I'm fine, Monsieur," she said, staring at her hand. A pinpoint of blood initialed the spot where the pin's clasp had pricked her skin. She curled her hand into a fist again, hiding the crimson dot that reminded her of the wash of blood that had darkened her vision. A vision that had seemed—felt, smelled, sounded—entirely real.

"Monsieur LaFayette, doesn't the Musée have Marie Antoinette's diaries and letters on file?" she asked, remembering what she had seen.

"We have them on microfiche, oui."

"May I look at them?"

"By all means, Mademoiselle."

Rachael rubbed the spot at the small of her back that ached interminably. She'd been studying the microfiche of Marie's writings all evening, but had only found the letter Marie had written to Yolande. At first she'd been startled, almost frightened to find something that confirmed her vision. But then she rationalized: surely in her studies she'd come across the letter before, and simply forgotten until her subconscious regurgitated it.

In all the 'fiches, she'd found no mention of the brooch. She'd hallucinated everything, of course. She hadn't eaten much that day; hell, she hadn't eaten much since becoming a starving student in France. Bread and cheese had become her usual sustenance. There was no way she could have seen Marie Antoinette and those events. The thrill of seeing and holding the brooch had sparked an already overactive imagination.

She arched her back, purring with pleasure as her vertebrae untwisted. Her mind, however, remained twisted around what happened, and yet couldn't have happened. The images had seemed so *real*, though; and not just images—all her senses had been violently, acutely involved. She glared at the microfiche reader, wishing she could lay the blame on it for not divulging the information she needed.

She'd started reading the diaries on the day the Cardinal was acquitted of wrongdoing in the Diamond Necklace Affair—a twist of fate that had stunned and angered Marie, Rachael knew—and worked her way forward, day by day. The going was slow; though she knew French well enough to get by during her stay here, the unfamiliar spelling and grammar of the language in the eighteenth century hampered her progress.

There must be some other way…. Rachael snapped off the machine and turned on the small reading lamp that squeezed a place for itself on the desk next to the machine. She flipped open the spiral notebook on her lap. She'd scribbled down everything she could remember about the brooch and her hallucination after she and Monsieur LaFayette had finished the inventory. Almost without thinking, she began to sketch the pin on the opposite page. Her hand seemed to work independently of her brain—a line here, a curve here, delicate shading there to give the illusion of facets in the jewel. The tiny flowers and curves of the etched design blossomed and swirled beneath the tip of her pen….

Rachael stared at the sketch, awed and a little frightened. She'd never been able to draw much more than stick figures, but the brooch seemed to glimmer from its place on the page. Perhaps it was the dim light? She leaned forward, somehow realizing that if she'd kept going, Marie would have come to life beneath her pen as well, soul flowing out with the ink to stain the paper with sorrow.

Maybe she'd been going about this the wrong way. A slow, tingling realization infused her. Shutting the book, she crossed the hall and stuck her head into the curator's office.

"Monsieur, was there a portrait done of Marie Antoinette to commemorate the birth of her daughter Sophie?"

The small man looked up from his paperwork and frowned thoughtfully, squinting as if to visualize the picture about which she asked.

"There was a small one commissioned when Sophie was three months old, Mademoiselle," he said. "The birth of a daughter was not a momentous occasion, of course, and the portrait is relatively insignificant. I have never seen it, and I am unsure of its exact date. If you think that is the one you mean, try the catalogues from the Musée de France—that is where the portrait of which I am thinking is hung."

Rachael gathered up the heavy catalogues from the bookcase and carried them, pressed possessively to her breast, back to the other room. She set the stack on the floor and settled the first one on her lap, tucking one leg beneath her as she sank into the chair. She leaned forward, trying to make the most of the light from the straining lamp.

Three catalogues to find it. Then, there it was: Marie, skin pale, dress blood-red as if to symbolize the blood that would someday spill. And at her throat, what had to be, despite the size of the reproduction, the brooch. She sat, one hand half-lifted to the jewel, a small smile on her lips, but a haunted, distant look in her eyes that had once been described as "imperial blue."

Rachael gripped the catalogue in suddenly sweat-slick hands, the chill down her back belying the moisture on her palms.

The picture proved nothing. It was too small to conclusively say the brooch was the one tucked away in the cabinet in the wine cellar, a masterpiece of topaz and gold languishing away in anonymity for simple lack of proof. The portrait itself would clinch it, but that was away in Paris, and she had to know now. *Now.*

Then she read the description next to the picture.

Of course. Portraits took more than a few days. She had to look in the diaries four months after Sophie's birth….

"I wore the lovely brooch from Yolande for the portrait sitting today. The painter commented on its beauty. Yolande was a dear to give it to me, but it will always remind me of the Cardinal and his forever unpunished treachery."

Searching back, Rachael found the entry where Marie spoke of receiving a brooch—a topaz-and-gold cross, described exactly like the one in the cellars—from her friend.

So it had really happened. She dropped the catalogue on the floor and drew her legs up into the chair, hugging her knees and rocking, ever so slightly, back and forth. Somehow, when she'd held the brooch, she'd been able to see the past, see directly into moments in its history.

One thought rose above the growing belief, the faint shock-fear and the swirling implications:

Would it happen again?

CHAPTER 1

October, seven years later

"HAVE A NICE VACATION, EH," the cab driver said, and heaved the suitcase over the lip of the trunk.

"Thanks," Rachael said absently, handing him the money, her eyes and thoughts on the grey-and-tan stone house before her. The faintest hint of apprehension trickled down her back, like a single bead of perspiration; then it was gone, swiped away by excitement and curiosity. She wasn't here for pleasure, but for work.

Behind her, the cab kicked into gear and motored off down the driveway that ribboned its way through a row of stately evergreens. And she heard, over the silence of the Adirondack Mountains, only the faint, distant purr of a lawn mower.

Manor MacPherson spread out before her, the late afternoon sun glinting off its many windows. The massive front door, located up a wide flight of low steps, was flanked by two bulging towers. On either side of the towers unfurled the wings of the house; except for the towers, the building was shaped like a capital I, because each wing ended in a front-to-back-facing hall.

Above the front door, in a semi-circle sweep of stained glass, Rachael saw the MacPherson family crest, a cat sejant, proper, and the words "Touch Not The Cat Bot A Glove." She wondered what had prompted the ancient MacPherson clan, far away and long ago in Scotland, to adopt such a warning for their motto: "Don't touch the cat without a glove."

The ominous motto somehow disturbed her, and she reminded herself that this was a job just like any other she'd had in the past few years. Simple genealogical research, back through the MacPherson family tree. She was eager to get started.

Hauling her laptop case and overstuffed suitcase up the steps, she opened the door and maneuvered inside. She stopped. Slowly setting the suitcase back down, she looked around, enchanted.

The front room was as fabulous as the outside of the house promised it would be. On either side, a massive stair-case began its ascent; halfway up, each split into two sets of stairs, heading forward and back to connect with walkways along the second floor. Above each staircase was a high skylight allowing a view of the wispy cirrus clouds outside. Hallways led left and right along the front of the house, as well as back beneath the staircases. Straight ahead were two pairs of paneled double doors, one door slightly ajar. A gilt chandelier hanging from the two-story ceiling provided crystalline flashes of light. The room smelled of fresh pine and a light, sweet scent Rachael couldn't identify.

There was no front desk, but a small sign beside a half-open door on the wall to her right said "Manager." Leaving her suitcase and computer inside the front door, Rachael crossed the parquet floor and peered in. A short woman, wearing a pinstriped blue-and-white blouse, khaki skirt, and Docksiders, was sliding a manila folder into a filing cabinet drawer. Rachael knocked lightly, and she looked up.

"Hi! Welcome to Manor MacPherson," the woman said, closing the drawer. Some of the freckles on her face vanished into the grooves of laugh lines around her eyes as she smiled. Rachael guessed her to be in her early thirties. "What can I do for you?"

"I'm Rachael de Young," Rachael said, extending her business card. Embossed in purple on the marbled lavender card were the words "Rachael S. de Young, Genealogical Researcher & Historian," and her contact information.

"You made it," the woman said, sounding pleased. "We've been looking forward to your arrival. Let me go tell Celeste you're here. I'm Karyn Cappricci, hotel manager, by the way." With barely a glance, she plucked a key from a pegboard and swung around the desk, her hip skimming the corner with practiced ease. "I'll be back in a sec—have a seat."

"Thanks," Rachael said, sinking into the indicated chair outside Karyn's office. But she'd been sitting all day—cab to plane to train to cab—and moments after Karyn had hurried off, she was up again, restlessly prowling the front room.

A host of MacPhersons had trod the floor where she walked, and she felt a heavy wave of history undulate beneath her feet. For a fleeting second she had the sensation of standing in the middle of all of them, as they surged and wandered and lived and died around her. Suddenly she felt as though she were no longer alone, and whirled. For the briefest of moments she thought she saw a pair of haunting green eyes, but she was still alone in the hall.

The MacPhersons, she knew, were known for the rich green of their eyes, and yet she couldn't shake the sensation that someone had been with her—not watching her, but being with her.

She was standing before a sweeping oil painting of what could only be the original Manor MacPherson in Scotland when Karyn returned to the front hall and returned Rachael to the present.

"I'm sorry, but Celeste is on an overseas business call," she said. "She'll be half an hour at most. Why don't I take you up to your room?" At Rachael's nod, she swept up the heavy suitcase. "Not only am I the manager, but I'm also the bell-hop," she said with a grin as she marched across the polished floor toward the right-hand set of stairs. Though her hips were roundly curved, she wasn't overweight or, obviously, out of shape. Rachael's long-legged stride allowed her to keep up with the energetic woman, and she was only one step behind as they mounted the staircase.

"I was really excited to hear you were coming," Karyn said, her blunt-cut pageboy swinging at her shoulders. "I studied history for a few semesters in college, and I wish I could have taken more classes in it."

"What kind of history did you study?" Rachael asked, now curious.

"Just your basic survey courses. I didn't have many free credits to blow, and history didn't have much to do with my major, Hotel Management. It was a real treat to get the job here—this place is fabulous."

"It is," Rachael agreed admiringly. She wished she could stop and look at every object, picture, and architectural feature that they passed, but she restrained herself, knowing she'd have ample time in the ensuing days.

"This wing, the east wing, is all guest rooms," Karyn explained, leading her down a long, narrow hall. "There are a few in the upper west wing, but most of that is the MacPher-sons' private living quarters. We're putting you in one of the business suites, since we figured you'd need some room to spread out your research stuff."

She had stopped about halfway down the hall, and, putting Rachael's suitcase down, inserted the large brass key into the lock. It turned easily, but Karyn had to use a shoulder to help encourage the heavy door to swing in. "Here you go," she said, standing back so Rachael could enter first.

The two-room suite enthralled Rachael, right down to the bowl of fresh flowers on the highboy and the crystal decanter of brandy and two glasses on the night table. She pulled her laptop out and set it on the desk, then slung the case back over her shoulder while Karyn laid her suitcase on the steamer trunk at the foot of the four-poster bed.

"Do you want to freshen up before you meet with Celeste?" the manager asked solicitously. "I know how tiring your trip must have been."

"No, I'm fine," Rachael said quickly. Her curiosity—what had led her to this field of study in the first place—demanded some immediate appeasement. "This is a huge house—how many rooms do you rent to guests?" she asked as she re-locked her door and pocketed the key in the comfortable jeans she'd worn for traveling.

"Twenty. We have eight regular rooms, four honeymoon suites, and six executive suites. We also have two rooms that each have an extra bedroom attached, in case a couple is traveling with a third person. We discourage small children, though—too many delicate antiques lying around."

As Karyn led her back downstairs, she pointed out the frescoes on the stairwell ceiling and the detailed carvings of the wall panels, which she said were exact copies of the origi-nals in Scotland.

"I'm also the tour guide," she joked. "I know as much about this house as Celeste and Ian do."

"What about the family history?" Rachael asked. "Are you an expert on that as well?"

Karyn paused on the landing. "If you're talking about the tragedy, then no. It's not discussed. Since you'll be researching the MacPherson history, I'm sure Celeste will speak to you about it." Her voice wasn't unfriendly, but held a firmness that Rachael knew better than to push. She wondered if Karyn fielded this question often, because of the guide book or simply local gossip. At any rate, Celeste had hired her, so she was the one to question.

"You can wait here, in the parlor," Karyn said, pushing the double doors open further so they could walk through into the room across the front hall. "Celeste will be with you in a jiff. If you need anything, I'll be in my office. Make yourself at home." She smiled and left.

Rachael dropped her attaché case on a settee and walked to the wide bay window. She knelt on the built-in, cushioned bench and looked out at the wide expanse of lawn, smooth as a putting green and dotted with small copses of trees and, Rachael saw with delight, a stone fountain. The lawn sloped away to a thicket of trees. With the afternoon sun upon them, the tops of the trees looked afire, the leaves crackling vermilion, pumpkin, and citron flames. And beyond the trees loomed the mountains that made up the Adirondacks. The majestic peaks ringed her vision, some tree-lined and colorful, others grey with shale and slate; the highest already snow-capped, fading into blue and purple in the distance. Rachael, a Midwestern-born-and-bred flatlander, never ceased to be awed by the presence of mountains, and her attention was only drawn away when she leaned farther into the oriel and saw the edge of a garden peeking out from the right side of the house. She couldn't wait to explore the grounds. But her first priority would be the massive house.

No, she realized ruefully as she slid off the bench, her

very first priority would be to find a bathroom. Finding her makeup kit, which was buried in the bottom of her attaché case, which doubled as her purse, she crossed the parlor to the door, and saw that Karyn's office door was shut. Well, she could certainly find a bathroom by herself.

"Pick a direction—any direction," she muttered cheerfully. Well, she'd been in the east wing already; perhaps it was time to explore the West. Karyn had said the family quarters were upstairs, but had given no indications that the lower level was private. She headed down the back corridor, carefully opening doors on both sides. She found two closets, a TV room, a staircase and two generic sitting rooms, and was beginning to give up hope when she discovered a short hall leading right, toward the back of the house. A whining noise caught her attention. That would mean a person, she deduced; she could ask on the whereabouts of the bathroom. She knocked, but no one answered; the whining clatter continued. She opened the door, and, surprised by what she found, she took an involuntary step inside.

Although the paneled walls, stained-glass window edging, hand-woven carpet and heavy dark furnishings definitely belonged to the manor, the rest of the office was thoroughly modernized; so much so that Rachael felt physically jolted. Two computers, each with a large, flat-panel LCD monitor, two printers (one a combo scanner/fax machine), and two telephones completed the high-tech array. The noise was from one of the printers, which was choking helplessly on a piece of paper. Rachael moved to succor the afflicted printer, tucking her makeup case under her arm. She opened the side of the printer, tugged at the paper, and it uncrinkled, revealing several more sheets that had built up in the mechanism.

And then someone grabbed her from behind.

Rachael cried out in surprise, a bright ribbon of fear

twisting and knotting itself about her midsection. Her makeup case tumbled to the floor. Heart pulsing frantically, she reached deep for strength and twisted in the powerful grasp, trying to free herself from the vise-like hands that gripped her upper arms.

"Don't turn around," a voice rasped close to her ear. Rachael smelled expensive, subtle aftershave and a hint of smoke—not cigarette, but more carbon-like, as if a match had suddenly flared. She stopped trying to crane her neck around, knowing if she continued, she would only anger her assailant.

"What are you doing in here? Don't you know this is a private office?"

From his words, Rachael realized this was no baseless attacker, but rather, a servant or security guard. She tried to determine why his voice contained the unnatural raspiness, wondering if he were trying to disguise it. His strong fingers bruised her biceps. She gritted her teeth and said, "I was looking for the bathroom. I heard a noise and saw that the printer was jammed."

"The bathroom is down the hall, second door on your left," he said shortly. He released one arm to swipe her makeup case off the floor. He handed it to her, then turned her and propelled her to the door. "Stay out of my office."

As he pushed her out of the room, she caught a glimpse of the hand that held her left arm. It was smothered in a supple black leather glove.

The door shut firmly, with finality; not a slam, but neither a soft click. Trembling, Rachael didn't stop walking until she was in the bathroom. Then she sat down.

By the time she'd finished washing her hands, they'd stopped shaking and she felt calmer. She'd intruded on the man's office, and of course he'd been angry. Yes, he'd been more forceful than the occasion warranted—he'd deliberately tried to frighten her, it seemed—but on the other hand, he'd walked in and seen a stranger messing with his printer. Still, she couldn't fathom why he'd not allowed her to see who he was.

A critical look in the mirror showed her that, as she'd expected, the hours of travel had done little to damage her makeup. Rachael found the stubby end of an eyeliner and brightened the line around her eyes in a cerulean that mirrored and accentuated her eyes. A few quick dabs of powder around her nose and on the slant of her high cheekbones completed her work, and she headed back to the parlor, hoping she hadn't missed Celeste.

Celeste was nowhere in sight, and Karyn's office door was still closed. Too shaken from her encounter with the strange man to sit and stare out the window, Rachael plopped down on the loveseat next to her attaché case and pulled out the heavy, banded folder that held her notes. She wrapped the wide rubber band around her wrist.

Northwoods Press
November 1, 19--

HEATHER MOUNTAIN, N.Y. — Tragedy struck last night at Manor MacPherson when fire ravaged an outbuilding, killing three family members and seriously injuring another.

Killed in the blaze were Jordan MacPherson; his brother, Shane MacPherson; and Shane's wife, Emilie Shaw MacPherson.

Mr. and Mrs. MacPherson's son, Ian, aged 6, is in critical condition at Mercy Hospital with burns on at least 50% of his body, hospital officials said.

Heather Mountain Fire Chief Wayne LeFevre said it is unknown at this time how the fire started in the unused cottage located approximately one-half mile from the manor.

The blaze was first noticed at about midnight by friends leaving the manor after the MacPhersons' annual All Hallows Eve Costume Ball.

By the time firemen put out the fire, the cottage was gutted.

Funeral arrangements for Misters MacPherson and Mrs. MacPherson are incomplete at this time.

No further details were available at press time.

Rachael practically had the words memorized, but the clippings still fascinated her, drawing her back again and again to read the blurred words. She fished in the folder for the next article.

Northwoods Press
November 3, 19--

HEATHER MOUNTAIN, N.Y. — The New York State Police have been called in to investigate the Manor MacPherson tragedy because they have learned two of the deceased were killed not by fire, but by gun shot.

Police have determined that Jordan MacPherson and his sister-in-law, Emilie Shaw MacPherson, were both shot sometime before the fire was started. Shane MacPherson, Mrs. MacPherson's husband and Jordan's brother, was not shot, police said. He was killed by the ensuing fire.

Fire officials continued their investigation today of the Manor MacPherson fire that destroyed an outbuilding on the manor property following the family's annual All Hallows Eve Ball.

"When we learned there had been a shooting as well, we started to look for signs of arson," said Fire Chief Wayne

LeFevre. Someone had spilled lamp oil around the building, a cottage located about one-half mile from the manor, he said.

Ian MacPherson, aged 6, remains in critical condition at Mercy Hospital. Dr. Joe Billings said he is unsure whether the boy will survive.

Due back at the manor today from New York City are Celeste MacPherson Jenner and her husband, Arden Jenner. The rest of the immediate family are currently in residence; letters have been dispatched to relatives in Scotland.

A wake will be held at Manor MacPherson on Friday and Saturday. Burial will be held at 3 P.M. Sunday at the family plot in Heather Mountain.

Rachel spoke into her digital recorder.

"Reminder: see if the State Police will release the investigation records. Also, see if the Heather Mountain Fire Department has records concerning the fire investigation. And see if the chief or any firefighters who fought the fire are still around."

The mysterious fire. In the past few years, Rachael had made a career of solving mysteries—of the genealogical type. She wasn't sure what intrigued her about unraveling family relationships and charting the place of people in history, but she did know she'd chosen a rather limited specialty in the field of history. While most of her colleagues found teaching jobs and worked to get grants for projects, or settled into jobs at museums or universities, Rachael had chosen to create her own niche.

The rest of the *Northwoods Press* articles she'd found contained little information, finally summarizing that police were baffled by the violent crime. The charred remains of a gun had been found in the shell of the cottage; it was believed to have been Shane's, but there was no way to tell who had fired it: whether someone had shot Jordan and Emilie with it or whether Shane tried to defend them. There were no clues pointing towards who might have set the fire. Young Ian, though badly scarred, had survived.

A sheet of heavy, cream-colored paper slipped from the folder as Rachael shuffled through the papers. The letterhead displayed the MacPherson family crest, and along the bottom was a strip of the MacPherson modern dress plaid, black, yellow, maroon and cream. Rachael fingered the fine stationery, looking at the bold strokes making up the signature of Celeste MacPherson Jenner, the person who had commissioned her for this project.

The matriarchal woman sat behind a wide desk topped with black slate, a Mont Blanc fountain pen poised in the act of signing the paper before her, a sheet of ivory stationery. An expensive perfume rose discreetly in the air.

"I've made up my mind," she said. "It needs to be done." Her voice held conviction, but her eyes were troubled. The person to whom she spoke stood before her; Rachael could only see his broad-shouldered back, and his hands where they rested on the edge of the desk—

—his left hand shrouded in a black leather glove.

The man began to turn....

Rachael gasped, the letter fluttering from her fingers. She pressed a trembling hand to her lips.

She hadn't meant for that to happen. She must be more tired than she realized—or more shaken by her confrontation. In the seven years since she'd discovered her psychic ability, she'd learned to control it. Images no longer came unbidden, unwanted, unexpected, when she held an object. But her control had just slipped, and the loss of restraint frightened her.

If she concentrated, Rachael knew she could learn a great deal about Celeste from this simple letter, including things that Celeste probably had no intention of sharing with her. She had already seen Celeste in her office in the act of signing the letter. She'd heard Celeste speak to the mystery man, smelt her perfume. That much, in a few meager seconds, from a single, simple piece of paper—and so much more was possible.

That, Rachael refused to do.

She was glad her talent for psychometry hadn't revealed itself until she was in her early twenties—when she was mature enough to deal with the implications of the power. If she decided to misuse her ability to see images by holding an object, she could delve into the most intimate and private matters a person had. Oh, occasionally the temptation was strong, as it had been when she returned from France to learn of her boyfriend's betrayal. But she'd swiftly decided that, when it came to that situation, what she didn't know wouldn't hurt her. And, she decided soon after, what she *could* know *could* hurt other people.

On the other hand, psychometry could be an extremely valuable tool for an historian. So Rachael had laid down a simple law for herself: Never use her psychometric powers on something that belonged to a living person. Sometimes that wasn't easy, for an object could be passed down through the generations, but, with practice, Rachael had learned how to focus her ability on the time period she was aiming for.

If the object had a particularly powerful event attached to it, however, images of that event might come unbidden, and she would struggle to retain her own identity and control the visions that swept her in. She had worked hard at that control, still knowing it would always be a frightening experience—consciousness snatched away, dropped into a pit where senses sharpened, experiences were unwanted and difficult to escape from. The recent shudder to her nerves had damaged her control as well.

The MacPherson project, she guessed, would be particularly difficult because the potent event had happened a mere forty years ago. The traces of memory of it would be fresh, unblurred by the passage of time, of hundreds of years of later memories pressed on top. Most of the recent history of the families she studied was relatively bland; usually the older events were more exciting. By the time Rachael handled them, the emotional aura on the objects had faded to a manageable level. But there was something about this project that had intrigued her from the moment she received Celeste's first letter.

Intrigued her—and frightened her. Frightened her in the same way that her slip when holding the letter frightened her. That was, Rachael realized, exactly why she had been apprehensive in the first place. The history of the fire hadn't been laid to rest yet, and she would no doubt continue fighting to keep herself from getting tangled in the strands of time.

She squared her shoulders. She was overreacting. She was here to study the entire MacPherson genealogy—the Halloween massacre was only a tiny part of their history, and not what she going to be spending her time on.

Despite everything, she *was* excited about this undertaking, and looked forward to spending some time in the beautiful Adirondack Mountains of upstate New York. Celeste MacPherson had said in the letter that autumn was the best time to visit the Adirondack Park. Rachael knew that the word "park" was a misnomer, bringing to mind tidy, open lands prepared for maximum visitation for city-dwelling vacationers; in reality, much of the alpine land was either privately owned or still in a state of untamed, often dangerous wilderness.

Although she'd never seen the North Country in the other seasons, Rachael had to admit she couldn't imagine a more beautiful setting than the one outside the bay window. Right now, a family of deer placidly munched their way across the lawn near the border of trees.

She shuffled through the papers on her lap, choosing not to reread the relatively unhelpful obituaries of Jordan, Shane, and Emilie, and selected a page she'd photocopied from a guidebook called *Where to Stay in Northern New York*. Pulling the rubber band from her wrist, she twisted it absentmindedly around her fingers as she read.

Manor MacPherson Built in 1850, this majestic hotel is one of the oldest buildings in the North Country. Copied almost to the stone from the historic MacPherson manor in Scotland, the hotel is still home to the MacPherson family. They opened to the public in 1956. Currently, Celeste MacPherson Jenner and her cousin, reclusive businessman Ian MacPherson, jointly run the operation. The MacPhersons also own MacPherson Syrup, Inc., one of the leading providers of maple syrup in the country.

There are few tales of ghosts or spirits at Manor MacPherson, despite a tragedy that the family steadfastly refuses to discuss. In 19--, three members of the family—Ian MacPherson's mother, father, and half-uncle—were killed one night: two by gunshot and the third in a mysterious fire, all in the same cottage on the property. Intense rumor at the time speculated that an illicit affair had been going on between two of the deceased, though no concrete evidence supports this. Some visitors to the manor say the faint notes of a piano are sometimes heard wafting from the music room when no one is inside—but it is doubtful that this romantic notion can be linked to the fire.

As if to divorce itself from that tragic night, the family still holds a gala, full-costume-required Halloween Ball every year, carrying on the family's hundreds-year-old tradition despite the fact that one took place on the night of the 19-- fire.

October is certainly a wonderful month to visit Manor MacPherson, not only for the sumptuous ball but also for the famous spectacle of fall leaves in the Adirondacks as well. Also to be noted is the foliage on Heather Mountain—the area was so named for the Scottish Highlands heather that the MacPhersons transplanted on their land when the manor was built. The hardy plants, blooming with sweet-scented flowers of purple, grey-blue and white, are another special touch that makes a stay at Manor MacPherson unique.

Manor MacPherson has managed to perfectly combine the brilliant architecture of the 1500s with the modern conveniences of the twenty-first century. Open an antique cupboard in your room and you'll find a hotpot, mugs, and a variety of imported teas atop a tiny fridge. Light switches are cleverly disguised to blend almost seamlessly with the surrounding woodwork....

"Rachael de Young?"

An older woman with impeccably coifed short white hair stood in the parlor doorway, smiling.

"Mrs. Jenner?" Rachael moved the overflowing file from her lap to the brocaded loveseat cushion so she could stand.

"Celeste, please," the woman said, coming forward and taking Rachael's hand between hers. "We can't have such formalities when we'll be working so closely together."

Rachael smiled back, feeling the last of her anxieties melt away before the gracious woman. She stuffed the photocopy back in the folder and shoved the whole thing into her attaché case.

"I'm sorry I kept you waiting," Celeste continued as they

left the parlor together. "It was a phone call that simply couldn't wait."

"No problem," Rachael said. The woman was several inches shorter than Rachael, and if it weren't for her snowy hair, her erect carriage and slim figure would easily cause her to be mistaken for a woman twenty years younger. Her navy suit and simple, high-necked red silk blouse spoke of both elegance and comfort. Rachael felt grubby in comparison in her jeans and soft grey knit shirt, but Celeste seemed not to notice—or if she did, she didn't mind. "It gave me a chance to look around a bit."

"And what did you think?" Celeste held open a door and allowed Rachael to enter first.

"Everything is beautiful—gorgeous," Rachael said lamely.

"Thank you, dear," Celeste said, and moved around to sit behind her desk.

Her black slate-topped desk.

At Celeste's gesture, Rachael sank into the comfortable burgundy-leather armchair across from her. So. Even unbidden, her visions continued to be accurate to the last detail.

A cluster of framed photos held court at one corner. Rachael tilted her head around to see them. Most were older, sepia-tinted. One, of a dark-haired man, struck her soul; even though the color couldn't be in the picture, she saw him with familiar eyes of green.

"Now, I do want to go over a few things before you get started on your research," Celeste said. "Let me give you a brief overview of the family. Of course, I will always be available to you—I'll give you whatever information I can. The rest of the family is to do the same, not that there are many of us left."

"You said that's the reason you wanted the family history charted," Rachael said. Celeste's office also contained modern computer equipment, but Rachael noted that it was recessed in the back wall and doors could be closed to hide it, better retaining the manor's antique charm.

"That's definitely one of the reasons," Celeste agreed. "Really, Ian and I are the only ones of this line, and we don't seem to be leaving any heirs. I've lost track of all the different groups in Scotland—you'll track most of them down, I'm sure—but I gather they're diminishing as well. Smaller families, fewer marriages, that sort of thing. My main interest, where I'd like you to concentrate, is on our line of the family since we came to America." She leaned forward. "Another reason, Rachael, is that, besides the manor itself, the one thing everyone knows about the MacPhersons is a tragedy we had here a number of years ago. I don't want that to be the only thing everyone remembers."

"The shootings and fire," Rachael supplied.

Celeste's green eyes narrowed. "You know about that?"

"Only because I did some research before I came here," Rachael said quickly, seeing the woman's discomfort. "I'd be a poor historian if I didn't do some preliminary study before I dove into a project."

"That's true," Celeste said, sounding relieved. "So, you know of our tragedy." She breathed in deeply, the sides of her aquiline nose hollowing. "Yes, I'll admit I'm sensitive about the subject—although not nearly as much as Ian is, poor boy." She paused, considering the neat arrangements of objects on her desk: leather blotter, pen holder, closed date book. "I don't want the only thing people remember about us to be that night, and especially not the rumors about it," she said slowly. "But I admit there's a concurrent reason why I hired you."

Rachael waited.

"In the course of your research, if you can, I wonder if you could find out who murdered three members of my family forty years ago."

CHAPTER 2

$\mathcal{E}$XCUSE ME?" RACHAEL GASPED. The warning flicker about this assignment that had been lurking in the back of her mind flared to life, Celeste's words like a piece of paper tossed on glowing embers. What, was she getting precognition to go along with the psychometry? What next? Spoon-bending? Reading auras? Astral projection?

"I'm sorry, Rachael, did I startle you?"

"A little," Rachael admitted. "I just don't understand—why do you think I could find anything more than the police did?"

Celeste rose and went to gaze out the window, which overlooked the back lawn that Rachael had been contemplating not long ago. The sun had nearly set, the blue of twilight overtaking the scene. A light in the base of the fountain turned the bubbling water to liquid crystal. The deer had gone.

"Let me tell you a little bit about my family," Celeste said finally. "My mother, Letitia, was twenty years older than her brothers, Jordan and Shane. As a result, I was seven years younger than Jordan and only five years younger than Shane; they were more like brothers to me....

"We had already left Manor MacPherson that night."

Rachael knew she meant the night of the shooting and fire.

"My husband and I were living in New York City, where he had a business. We had come up for the Halloween Ball, but left on the last train out that night because Arden had an important meeting the next morning. Of course, we came back as soon as we heard the news."

Rachael remembered reading that Celeste's husband had died about a year ago. She wondered if that had sparked Celeste's interest in the family geneology.

Celeste turned and walked back to her desk, sitting and folding her hands before her. Her short, carefully manicured nails shone with a clear polish.

"As the youngest member of the family, and a woman to boot, I wasn't privy to much of what went on in the higher echelons of the household." She laughed shortly, derisively. "I was, however, a good listener. I still am. I heard the rumors, and I heard the whisperings of my family, and I put two and two together." Her eyes, hued the legendary MacPherson green, ensured Rachael's attention. "You've done your homework, so you know what some of the rumors were. I believe my family preferred there not be an intense investigation into the murders. I don't know if they were protecting anyone—perhaps it was simply the family honor."

Celeste smiled, a bit sheepishly, and Rachael nodded for her to continue.

"I thought that since you're already here doing research on the family, you might be able to find some answers," the older woman said. "Oh, I may be being foolish; sentimental and suspicious in my old age. But I truly would like to know what happened that night. Lay the ghosts to rest."

"Do you believe there are ghosts?" Rachael asked, remembering the tour book's offhand comment.

Celeste laughed. "Oh no, my dear, that was a figure of speech. I don't believe in spooks and spirits. I'd like to know more about my ancestors, but I don't expect them to come back themselves to tell me." She sobered. "Rachael, I would appreciate it if you didn't recount our discussion to Ian," she said. "As you must know from your research, he was seriously injured in the fire." At Rachael's nod, she went on. "Apparently he saw someone—his father or mother, probably—head to the cottage, and he snuck away from his nanny to follow. He was caught in the fire, and seriously burned on half of his body. The scars, both physical and mental, can never be erased.

"Because of his disfigurement, Ian has been tutored at home all his life. He even graduated from college with the highest honors through studying at home. Modern technology has allowed him to run his business activities and transactions from his office here in the manor. If a situation demands his presence, he sends a stand-in. He is well-known and well-respected in the business community, but never seen."

Celeste toyed with the black Mont Blanc pen in its holder. "Ian is very self-conscious about the way he looks, of course. But you're a mature woman, Rachael; I don't think you'll have any problem seeing beyond Ian's scars."

"I'm very impressed by what he's accomplished," Rachael said honestly. "It is a true testament to his spirit and drive that he has achieved what he has. I respect hard work and intelligence in anyone."

"Good for you." Celeste rose again. "I don't know how much help Ian will be to you with regard to the fire," she said as she moved around the desk. "He never speaks of it; says he can't remember, which is common in trauma cases like that, I understand. I can't imagine a child going through such an event without experiencing great shock. No matter how long ago it was, it must still bring him great pain."

"Perhaps it would be best if I let him bring up the subject," Rachael said, gathering up her bag. "He knows why I'm here—he may volunteer some information eventually."

"He might," Celeste said as they walked to the door. "We can speak about this some more at a later time. I hope that you'll have dinner with us tonight, Rachael. Guests dine separately, but as you'll be working here, I'd like you to get to know us. Karyn will be dining with us as well—we consider her part of our little family."

"I'd like that," Rachael said.

"Dinner will be at seven o'clock. We don't dress too formally, but you'll want to wear a skirt. We put out a buffet of hors d'œuvres in the parlor at six thirty; you'll be able to meet some of the other guests then."

"That sounds lovely," Rachael said, and they parted ways.

She hadn't realized how travel-grimy she felt until she'd stripped off her clothes. She found her toiletry kit and hair dryer, and carried both into the adjoining bathroom. That room was dominated by a huge, claw-footed white porcelain bathtub. Rachael noted with delight the basket of bath beads, soaps, and powders on a stool near the tub.

The plumbing at the manor was definitely modern. Water cascaded over her, the pounding spray attaining the high temperature she preferred. Lathering up a loofah, she mentally replayed her meeting with Celeste MacPherson Jenner. She found that now, upon reflection, she felt less surprised by the woman's request. She was, after all, a historian, trained in research. If the family had suppressed an investigation into the fire, then she wouldn't have much to go on; then again, with the family pressure turned off, someone might be willing to divulge some long-secret information.

There was another possibility for Celeste's entreaty, however. Biting her lip, Rachael wondered if somehow, impossibly, Celeste knew about her power. If she did, she would certainly believe Rachael was capable of solving the forty-year-old, hushed mystery.

But there was no way Celeste could know, because Rachael had never told anyone of her gift. Whenever she came close, whenever she was tempted to ease the burden by revealing its existence to another, she closed her eyes and visualized the tabloid headlines. She would not, absolutely would *not* allow herself to be known as one of those sleazy psychics who solved murders, tracked down missing children, pointed police in the direction of criminals.

After the surprise of discovering her psychometry had worn off, after she'd returned home from France, Rachael had been woken night after night by dreams of people chasing her, clawing at her, begging her to find their children, their wedding rings, the treasure they were sure their ancestors had hidden: "Touch the handkerchief—oh please, this watch—can you see if you hold these strands of hair—?" They wept, they pleaded, they cajoled, they threatened. They wouldn't stop until she appeased them, and then others would take their places, crying out for the same help; the stories differed, but the desired end was the same. They beat upon her until she acquiesced, and more came and demanded until Rachael dropped of exhaustion. She would wake shivering in her bed, more tired than she had been when she lay down, feeling physically pummeled and sore.

Those nightmares had been interspersed with dreams of cowering as others taunted her as a freak, a crazy, a psycho. Even the gentle faces of her parents would surface, swimming to the forefront, their eyes questioning and fearful.

So Rachael had rented a cabin on Nag's Head for a weekend, and sometime Saturday night, in the dream-suppressing haze of vodka, she had sworn to herself that she would tell no one. She accepted the power, agreed with herself to use it discreetly in her work and never for personal gain.

The dreams never returned.

Rachael wondered if Ian had had such nightmares, or worse, had experienced the taunting, the pity or the fear. He hadn't been born with his scars, they had been thrust upon him as her power had been thrust upon her. But unlike her, he had no way to hide them.

A trail of conditioner tickled down her cheek, breaking Rachael from her reverie. No, there was no way Celeste could know of her psychometry; there was no reason for her to panic. She was tired, and feeling vulnerable; that was all.

After her shower, she put on her favorite dress, a comfortable turtleneck that hugged her upper figure and flared out at the waist. She knew the teal blue brought out her eyes and the form-fitting cotton knit accentuated her slim waist. She worked hard at her figure, having inherited her mother's bountiful bosom and thus the tendency to gain weight, despite slim hips gained from her father's side of the family. Rachael was unable to resist a twirl before the mirror, flaring the calf-length skirt nearly to her stocking-tops…but in mid-twirl her ankle twisted and she nearly fell, catching the wall just in time.

"Damn heels," she muttered as she eased into the chair in front of the floral-skirted dressing table. She crossed one leg over the other and glared at the black, spike-heeled pump. She grasped the heel, and it wiggled obligingly. "Damn," she repeated. She made mental note to take it in to a shoe repair shop in town, and leaned forward to apply her makeup. A silver Victorian-inspired necklace and matching heart-shaped earrings, a jingling cluster of bangle bracelets at her left wrist, and her grandmother's silver-and-diamond ring on her right hand, and she was ready.

She didn't hurry downstairs; instead, she lingered, admiring the manor and all its intricacies: the ornate carvings, the surprises of tiny portraits and landscapes tucked in unusual nooks, the occasional well-placed antique chair or table. An object propped on a built-in shelf caught her eye, and she paused to examine it. It was an old cloak pin: a crest badge, and a MacPherson one at that; Rachael could just make out the faint letters of the motto on the curve of the gold circle. After a brief hesitation, she picked it up. She needed to find out whether she was back in control of her power.

Cupping the cloak pin in her palms, Rachael stared at it until she had its curves and clasp memorized. Closing her eyes, she pictured the pin, and hefted its weight in her hands, the metal heavy and cool. Then, carefully, she blanked her mind of all thoughts and opened herself to whatever might come.

The room smelled of tallow and peat, of unwashed bodies—and of death. By the fire it was warm, but the rest of the room felt cold and damp. The fire provided the only illumination, for it was twilight outside the small, unshaded window.

A man lay on a pallet, eyes shut, unmoving. A woman gently unfastened the cloak pin from his woolen wrap and straightened, turning to face a young boy of no more than fifteen, his face pale beneath his shock of red hair. He stood, back straight, as his mother pinned the badge to his cloak with trembling fingers.

"You're the eldest, now, Ewen," she said, her eyes bright with unshed tears. Rachael had to struggle to understand her words, garbled by her thick brogue. "You're the laird of our house. We'll send word to th'MacPherson in the morn."

Rachael let out a whoosh of air and opened her eyes, blinking to reorient herself in the brighter-lit hallway, and the present. She gently replaced the pin on the shelf. She longed to retreat to her room, find the art pad and colored pencils as yet unpacked, and dust the fine freckles on the boy's cheeks. Though she had no real talent for art most times, after she used her power she found she could render the scene in exquisite precision, often revealing details she hadn't noticed.

Realizing she was now late, Rachael hurried the rest of the way down the hall to the staircase. Halfway down the stairs, she paused on the landing, listening. Subtle music drifted out of the parlor between the open double doors; she identified the faint droning wail of bagpipes. From this angle she couldn't see inside, but she heard the murmur of voices as well. She quickly started down the last flight of stairs.

And then the heel of her shoe snapped. Rachael felt herself pitching forward and grabbed frantically for the banister, her stomach lurching. Her fingers skidded along the finely polished wood, unable to gain purchase. She cried out.

A firm hand grasped her elbow, stopping her fall, hauling her upright. She clutched at the banister again, and this time, steadied, she managed to grab hold of it. Gasping, she gripped the sturdy wood with both hands, and turned to thank her savior.

No one was there. She could see both flights of stairs after they split, and there was no way someone could have gotten down one of the hallways before she turned. She slowly sat down.

"Rachael, are you all right?"

The voice was Celeste's. The woman had emerged from the parlor. Several other faces peered from the room in consternation.

"I'm fine—my heel broke, and I stumbled," Rachael said, willing her heart to slow its incessant drumming. She held up the offending shoe; the heel dangled. She took a deep breath. "I'm fine."

The other faces receded politely. As she approached the doors, Celeste asked, "You're sure you're fine?"

Rachael nodded. "I need to go get another pair of shoes."

"No, you rest for a moment. Maria?"

The black-and-white clad servant paused in the doorway to the parlor, looking up at them.

"Could you run an errand for me, please?" Celeste asked. Maria passed her tray of shrimp cocktail to another maid in the parlor and came up the stairs to where they were. Rachael described the shoes she wanted, and gave Maria her room key and the pumps.

"You're still pale," Celeste said. "Would you care for a drink?"

Rachael requested a whisky sour, and when Maria returned, Celeste passed the order on to her. The servant, her reddish-brown hair caught in a neat hairnet, smiled and hurried off.

"How many people do you have working here?" Rachael asked, slipping on the lower-heeled burgundy pumps.

"Nancy Rabideau is in charge of the staff, as well as being our full-time cook," Celeste answered as they walked down the stairs and across the front hall. "Her husband, George, is the groundskeeper. You've already met Karyn, of course. We hire out for daily maids and other servants."

As they entered the parlor, Maria arrived with her drink. Rachael smiled and thanked her.

"Now, let me introduce you to the other guests," Celeste said.

Rachael made brief small talk with all the people currently staying at Manor MacPherson. Doug and Ally, the honeymooners, giggled and said hello and went back to their contented murmuring at one another. Businessmen Brian,

David, and Kevin each shook her hand gravely and then delved back into their quiet, earnest discussion; and William and Janet, a couple from nearby Plattsburgh who were celebrating their twenty-fifth anniversary, welcomed her to upstate New York.

"A couple from Alabama will be arriving Sunday," Celeste added after they had made the rounds. "Then there'll be a brief lull before the All Hallows Eve Ball crowd."

Rachael sipped her drink, feeling the alcohol warm and relax her. "You keep busy," she commented.

"We try," the older woman said, surveying the group. "Guests are the lifeblood of a hotelier, of course."

They chatted for a few minutes, and then dinner was announced. The guests filed into the formal dining room, and Celeste led Rachael to where the family would be having their supper.

If this is the small *dining room....* Rachael thought, gazing around the expansive room. The white vaulted ceiling was crossed with dark beams, and a dark, carved wooden screen half-hid a door on the side wall that probably led to the kitchen area. A tapestry on the back wall depicted, appropriately, a medieval feast scene. A long heavy table dominated the room, a drape of milky lace upon it. The table was set with Bird of Paradise china and a delicate crystal that glittered in the light provided by an overhead chandelier, carefully dimmed, and candles on the sideboards and dining table.

Rachael was several steps into the room before she realized there was someone already seated at the rectangular table; at the long end, away from the door. His profile was to the women as they entered, the candles causing his silhouette to flicker. He was studying something on his lap, pausing only to type some figures into the calculator that sat on the table next to him; his plate had been pushed aside to accommodate the small machine.

"Ian," Celeste said affectionately as they walked toward him, "Can't you set aside your work long enough for dinner?"

"I was just going over a few figures before everyone else showed up," he said, his fingers swiftly tapping. He examined the calculator's display out of the corner of his eye, made a notation on the paper on his lap, then flicked off the machine. He slid something, which seemed to be a book of matches, off the table and into his jacket pocket.

"Ian, this is Rachael de Young, the historian I hired."

"Ms. de Young." Ian stood, and, smiling, extended his right hand.

Rachael was glad Celeste had prepared her for Ian's looks. She could imagine how it must hurt him when people unwittingly flinched at the sight of the shiny, puckered skin on the left side of his face. He had grown his hair longer and combed it down to cover the burned area on the side of his scalp where no hair now grew. No left eyebrow remained, and the scars tugged up at the left corner of his mouth. The burn scars continued down his neck until they disappeared into the starched collar of his shirt. His left hand was shrouded in a black leather glove.

"Good evening, Mr. MacPherson," Rachael said calmly, returning his firm grip, remembering how his hands had painfully gripped her arms and shoved her from his study.

"I'd like to apologize for my actions earlier this evening," he went on. "I didn't realize who you were."

"That's quite all right," Rachael replied. "I can imagine how it must have looked to you, finding me fiddling with your printer."

"I hadn't realized you two had met," Celeste said, looking from one to the other.

"We ran into each other earlier, briefly, when I was waiting for you," Rachael said quickly, not wanting to embarrass Ian by relating the whole story. Before she could continue, however, another voice called out,

"Oh, dearie me, I'm not late, am I?"

Rachael turned to see a petite, elderly woman enter the dining room. She walked with a cane, but seemed to be using the instrument not as crutch, but as a way to propel herself faster toward them.

"No, Felicity, you're not late," Celeste said warmly. "Come and meet Rachael."

"Rachael!" The woman took one of Rachael's hands between hers. Rachael expected frail hands, but instead felt wiry strength beneath the papery, cool skin. The woman's green eyes were bright and seemed to regard her—and the rest of the world—with bemused contentment. Paint, bright orange, smudged her cheek. "How good of you to come! I'm Felicity MacPherson. You must call me Felicity—don't be stuffy just because I'm old; I won't stand for it."

"Thank you, Felicity."

"Felicity is my aunt—she and my mother were twins—and Ian's half-aunt," Celeste explained. "She's an artist."

"So I gathered," Rachael said.

"Whoops!" Felicity looked down at the paint-spattered smock she still wore. Leaning her cane against a chair, she reached behind and untied the apron. She looked around thoughtfully, then opened the credenza along the side wall, wadded up the smock and tossed it inside. Shutting the door, she leaned against the credenza with an innocent smile that was negated by the wicked twinkle in her eyes.

Celeste cleared her throat. "Felicity is quite well known in the Adirondack area, as well as central New York and Vermont. She had several shows in New York City that were rather successful."

"You might want to include some of Felicity's work in the volume of family history," Rachael suggested, delighted by the whole interchange.

"That's a lovely idea," Celeste agreed. "I had been considering a gorgeous oil she did of the manor."

Maria slipped into the room through a back door and informed Celeste that the guests had been served.

"Please tell Nancy we'll wait a few more minutes," Celeste told her. "Karyn hasn't arrived yet."

"Rachael, may I refresh your drink?" Ian asked. At her nod, he took her empty glass to the row of crystal decanters on the far sideboard. She noticed that he walked with a slight limp, as if the left side of his body were stiff. When he returned, she sipped the cold, sour drink and asked him about the business of running a hotel. He was describing their different forms of advertising when Karyn hurried into the room.

"I'm sorry I'm late," she said breathlessly. "Brett's sitter cancelled at the last moment, and I had to drive him to a friend's house in town. Brett's my son," she added for Rachael's benefit. "I'm also a mother," she said with a grin, continuing her earlier listing of her duties.

"You don't live in town?" Rachael asked.

"Karyn and Brett, as well as Nancy and George, live in cottages on the grounds," Celeste supplied. Seeing Maria peering into the room, she nodded at the servant's unspoken question. "Why don't we sit down?"

They clustered at one end of the long table, Ian at the head, Celeste on his left and Felicity to his right. Ian poured everyone wine as Maria and a plump, middle-aged woman, who was introduced to Rachael as Nancy Rabideau, brought in the first course, a crisp green salad with bright cherry tomatoes and Roquefort dressing.

The conversation flowed with the wine, enhancing each

course of the meal. Karyn asked Rachael about her work, and so Rachael found herself at the center of attention during most of supper. Everyone seemed honestly interested in her career, although she noticed that Ian grew quiet when she discussed the family studies she had done.

"It seems to me," he said finally, "that the past is the past. What do we really gain by spending so much time and energy studying it? Isn't it better to look to the future, work toward it?"

He didn't speak antagonistically, and Rachael wasn't offended by his questions. He brought up a debate in which even historians took sides.

"Some say we can learn about the future from studying history," she said, dabbing cream sauce from the corner of her mouth with her napkin. "You know the old idea: that we must learn from our mistakes or forever repeat them."

He set his fork gently onto the china dinner plate. "But isn't it better to learn from our own mistakes, instead of trying to interpret someone else's?"

"You've got a point," Rachael said, warming to the debate. "The farther we go back in history, the harder it is to learn exactly what happened. The outcomes are easy to see, but it's harder to determine what caused them."

"Let the past be the past—let it rest," he said.

"Ian," Celeste said.

"'The circumstances are in a great measure new. We have hardly any landmarks from the wisdom of our ancestors to guide us,'" Felicity quoted. "Edmund Burke," she added as they all looked at her, and popped an asparagus tip into her mouth.

"Felicity," Celeste said in the same tone of voice she had directed at Ian.

"Oh no, that's okay," Rachael said quickly. "I've had this sort of discussion many times before. Many people feel the way Ian does. Unfortunately, sometimes those are the people holding the grant money."

Karyn and Felicity chuckled, and even Celeste had to smile.

"Well, what Rachael does is different," she said. "Researching a family's genealogy is a way to make the past relevant."

"I don't agree," Ian said. "In fact, I see less of a point in finding out that, oh, one's ancestor owned twenty head of cattle or fought in the Battle of Hastings."

Rachael chewed a piece of chicken, savoring the creamy wine sauce. "Some people simply find it interesting," she said. "For others, it's a matter of pride to be able to say their great-great-great-whoever came over on the *Mayflower*."

"I've always felt our ancestors helped shape who we are today," Karyn spoke up.

"What a lovely way of phrasing it!" Celeste said. "That's exactly what I was thinking—I've just never been able to put it into words."

"I like to believe I've shaped myself." Ian looked up. He rolled his knife between his fingers; candlelight glinted off the blade. The scars on the left side of his face seemed to pulse a deeper red. "I am who I am because I've worked, and struggled, and learned—and yes, failed, and learned from my own mistakes. My great-great-great-whoever had very little to do with it."

"'People will not look forward to posterity, who never look backward to their ancestors,'" Felicity said complacently. "Also Burke."

"Then you're not in accordance with Celeste on this project?" Rachael asked Ian.

He set down the knife carefully, the end of the blade resting on his plate. "Celeste and I discussed the matter at length before you were hired," he said finally. "While I may not be in total agreement on the necessity or value of this research, I will give you my full cooperation." He smiled slightly. "I was overruled, but that doesn't mean I'm not a graceful loser. Please don't hesitate to come to me with questions, Rachael. I do want to help you."

"Thank you," she said. The strained atmosphere escaped out the door as Nancy and Marie brought in the dessert, a fresh fruit sorbet and slices of spongy, light pound cake.

After supper they retired to one of the sitting rooms Rachael had found on her quest for the bathroom. Large mirrors on the walls, gilt-framed, made the room seem larger without reducing its intimacy. The fireplace held a careful placement of birch logs, a fire unnecessary this early in the season.

Finally feeling the effects of her day of traveling, Rachael declined an after-dinner crème de menthe and chose another cup of coffee instead. The French vanilla aroma was rich and comforting.

Celeste asked Rachael where she would be starting her research.

"I'd like to interview each one of you," she answered. "You'll all have different memories, have heard different stories about the past. I'd also like to go through whatever family papers are available. After that, I'll see about getting whatever certificates—birth, marriage, death—and other official documents. My first goal is to put together as complete a family tree as I can, and then work on details from there."

"I know there's a family Bible in the library," Celeste mused. "I'll see what else I can find."

"Why don't I give you the full tour of the manor on Sunday?" Karyn suggested. "I should have the afternoon free after the Alabama couple check in. They're due at one, I think."

"Didn't Grandfather have a file of papers in his office that were related to the family?" Ian spoke up.

"I think you're right," Celeste said. "Can you find that?"

"I'll try. You know how Grandfather's study is."

Celeste turned to Rachael. "The man had a truly unique filing system," she said.

"If you don't mind, I'd love to look through his files myself," Rachael said. "There's no telling what may crop up. No offence, but you might not know if something was important or not," she said to Ian. "I've learned the hard way that anything can be useful: a receipt, a scribbled note, a ticket stub…."

"No offence taken," Ian said. "I'll look for that particular file, and you can go through the study later, at your leisure."

Rachael felt a yawn coming on, and her coffee cup clinked in the saucer as she hastily set it down and covered her mouth. "Well," she said with a laugh, "if I'm going to get any work done tomorrow, I'd best get myself to bed."

"I'll walk you to your room," Ian offered, and she accepted. She said goodnight to the others, and they left.

"I want to apologize for my actions this afternoon," he said. "I had no idea who you were."

"It was my fault as well," Rachael said. "I shouldn't have gone into your office uninvited."

"I overreacted," he said. "We should just agree to forget it happened."

"Good plan."

They lapsed into silence, Ian so silent that Rachael thought he was brooding. She noticed that he made a point of walking at her left, so his unscarred side was presented to her.

"I hope I didn't offend you with my remarks at dinner," he said suddenly. "I was in no way trying to demean your work."

"I wasn't offended," she assured him. "You presented some valid points. I'd rather debate with you than to argue with some pig-headed fool who doesn't even listen to what I'm saying."

He smiled. "I meant what I said—I'll help you in any way I can. Though I don't think I'll be much of a source for you."

"You might be surprised," Rachael said. "If you spent any time with your grandparents, you might remember some of the stories they told you."

They began the ascent of the stairs, Rachael discreetly slowing down so Ian wouldn't overextend himself.

"I won't be much help to you with regard to the night of the fire," he said suddenly. "I remember nothing."

"Celeste told me," Rachael admitted.

"I know that you will have to include that night in your research, because it is a part of our history," he said. She could hear the tension in his voice, saw the way his shoulders tightened beneath his suit jacket. "But I ask you not to dwell upon it." They were nearly to her room, and Rachael was already reaching into her small handbag for her key when he swung to face her, placing his hands lightly on her arms. "That part of the past is very painful for me—for the whole family. There is no need for you to do more than mention it in the book. That night did not shape me: I shaped myself from what remained of me after the incident. And there is nothing to be learned from the past."

"I understand," Rachael said. It was best not to argue with him, nor to agree and have him challenge her work later. "My job here is research. While I intend to produce as complete a history of your family as I can, I don't want to hurt anyone."

His shoulders dropped slightly, and he let her go. "Thank you. Good night, Rachael."

She put her shoulder to the door and bumped it open. "Good night, Ian."

The room was dark; but then, neither man needed light to know the other was there. One could sense the other's presence, and the other needed no light to see.

"She has power," one said. "Strong power."

"I know," the other said. He stared out the window. Soft fingers of clouds lovingly caressed the cold half-circle of the moon.

"You will not harm her," the first man said evenly. His words nonetheless conveyed a subtle threat.

"I will not let her learn the truth," the second man said. There was the barest hint of desperation in his voice. His fist clenched. "I *cannot*."

"But you will not harm her," the first man repeated, his words a cold presence. "I will not allow that."

END OF PREVIEW

What Beck'ning Ghost is available in print or ebook from all your favorite retailers.

WAKING THE WITCH
PREVIEW

What happens when four boys confess to the murder of a woman who died a hundred years ago...?

The violent encounter Rowan Everly survived in college jolted awake her psychic power to see past images while holding a related object. At the behest of a friend, she comes to the privileged prep school town of Millburn, New York, to investigate the current rape and murder, and hopefully clear her friend's son's name.

Rowan's not sure she's up to the task. Her deeply ingrained mistrust of men makes her question where her loyalties lie. The deeper she investigates, the less anything makes sense. The boys seem truly horrified by what happened—almost as if they hadn't had control over it.

Her initial encounter with sheriff Toby Candusco isn't pleasant for either of them. But his calm support of her, and his unwavering desire to see justice done, gives her the strength to not only face her fears, but to reexamine the core beliefs that shape who she is.

Only then can she face and destroy the real menace…and save everyone around her.

Turn the page for a sample of *Waking the Witch*, an atmospheric gothic mystery from Dayle A. Dermatis.

<h1 style="text-align:center">CHAPTER 1</h1>

IF SHE HADN'T been so exhausted by the red-eye from San Francisco to JFK, Rowan's psychic shields wouldn't have been down when Chloë met her at the train station in Poughkeepsie.

One minute she was stepping out of the station, juggling her bags and breathing in the crisp autumn air, and the next she was being swept up in a fierce hug.

"Oh God, Rowan, thank you for coming."

Normally she would never pry, never try to sense something personal without permission, but Chloë had caught her off guard. Rowan slammed the lid on her sixth sense and returned the hug.

"Of course. Anything for you. You said it's about Bryson?"

"Yes. God. I couldn't talk about it on the phone. Not here, either. Let's get your bags into the car."

Under other circumstances, Rowan would have been delighted to see Chloë. It had been nearly a year since they'd seen each other, when they'd been bridesmaids at the wedding of Amanda, the third member of their college suite.

That celebration had taken place six months after Chloë had married David and moved to Duchess County, New York.

Rowan had been skeptical when Chloë first enthused about her new paramour. David was twenty years older than Chloë, a divorcé with a teenage son, and decidedly wealthy. Chloë wasn't the type to be swept off her feet by money, and Rowan couldn't quite understand what the attraction was; plus she and Amanda worried that David was merely looking for a trophy wife or a permanent nanny for his son.

At Amanda's wedding, though, Rowan had had to admit that she'd never seen Chloë happier. David had set up a sculpting studio for her and she was preparing for her first big show. They were obviously in love, always holding hands and exchanging kisses, both enthusiastic about trying to create a half-sibling for sixteen-year-old Bryson.

But now, sitting in the car on the way from the station, Rowan saw a huge change brought on by the strain of recent events. Pasty-skinned and hollow-eyed, Chloë looked as though she hadn't slept in days, which she probably hadn't. Was it possible to lose weight so quickly? Rowan wondered, looking at Chloë's hands as she deftly turned the steering wheel of her gleaming silver Saab turbo. The extravagant diamond-and-emerald engagement ring seemed to be sliding around on her thin finger.

"Thank you for coming, Rowan," Chloë said again. "I can't tell you how much it means to me."

"You know I'll always be there for you," Rowan said. "Just tell me what I can do."

Chloë flashed her a wan smile. "Just moral support right now, love. And a little stability in a world gone mad."

Then, as if granted a sudden surge of energy, she wrapped her fingers around Rowan's wrist, her grip as tight and as desperate as her hug had been. "I need you," she said, "to use your powers and find out if he really did kill someone."

"Isn't it a little early for drinks?" Rowan asked.

She'd indulged in a nap, needing to be at her best for what she guessed she had to do soon. Still, it was only early afternoon. The housekeeper had put together a seafood salad and left out crusty rolls, lettuce, and tomato, as well as apple crisp and fresh whipped cream, but they'd only nibbled. Chloë said she wasn't ready to talk just yet.

Now she was, with, apparently fortification.

"Yes," Chloë said. "But we'll need it. Scotch, still?"

The bar was behind the sofa, so Rowan murmured a response rather than nodding. She slipped off her shoes and tights, and stretched her bare feet towards the fire, her fuchsia-lacquered toenails shimmering in the light of the flames. From hidden speakers, Celtic New Age mood music provided a soothing backdrop.

The room's décor wasn't what she would have expected of Chloë, but she knew that Chloë had been loath to make major changes when she moved in, not wanting to disrupt David's or Bryson's home too much. Still, Rowan could see some touches that were definitely her friend's: the Waterhouse "Siren" print on the wall, the Salomé statue on the mantle.

Chloë handed her a cut-crystal glass of single-malt Talisker—just a finger—and settled on the burgundy leather sofa next to her with a white wine spritzer. And they finally talked about what had happened.

"A group of men gang-raped a girl and left her to die." Chloë said it all in a rush, as if needing to get it out before something choked her. She gulped at her drink and set down the glass. "The next morning, they all confessed. Only they weren't men—they were high school boys. Including Bryson."

She did crumble into tears then, and Rowan held her, murmuring words of strength and smelling the expensive shampoo in Chloë's silky hair. What must it be like, Rowan wondered, to have your son confess to rape? For Chloë had adopted Bryson and by all her accounts adored him, as he did her.

Chloë's sobs subsided. "I know things like this have happened before: upstanding, hard-working kids who nobody thought could do any wrong. Or the parents are too high-and-mighty to accept that their child could have done such a thing, or even if he did he must be protected at all costs." She shook her head. "I know I sound like one of those." Her red-rimmed eyes pleaded with Rowan. "But I swear, I *do* know Bryson! I *do* know he would never rape somebody! I mean, he's absolutely sick over what's happened."

"There is such a thing as mob mentality," Rowan said slowly, carefully. "Caught up in the heat of the moment, egged on by your peers…"

Chloë scraped back her blond hair. The short, classic cut was a far cry from the pink-and-blue spikes she had favored in college. "I know," she admitted, her voice tiny. She raised her glass to her mouth again, and Rowan did the same, feeling the burning of the Scotch chase its way down her chest. "But…it's the same thing with all the boys. I know them—maybe not well, but they've all been friends for years, and I do know their parents. They all seem…horrified— sickened, even—at what's happened. At what they've— they've—"

"At what they've done?" Rowan finished.

Her friend shook her head again, her green eyes suddenly stubborn. "At what they've *confessed to doing*," she rephrased firmly. "That's the strangest part, don't you see? They've confessed to raping this girl, but so far, none of the physical evidence incriminates them. In fact, so far it absolves each and every one of them."

"How so?"

"Nothing found at the scene links the boys to even being there. Not hair, nor clothing scraps, nothing. None of the boys had any unusual scratches or bruises that would indicate a struggle. Only one of them physically seemed to have, ah…" Chloë glanced towards the fire, obviously searching for the right word. "…seems to have been sexually active the night before, and as near as the doctor who examined him can tell, he wasn't…active with anyone else."

"Got it," Rowan murmured.

"Obviously, they could have showered afterwards, so that fact in and of itself doesn't say much," Chloë continued. "Meanwhile, none of the boys had ever shown a propensity towards anger or violence. Yes, two of them are on the football team, but nothing beyond just playing the game. Two of them have girlfriends, and both girls have gone on record saying the boys had never been abusive or rough with them."

Rowan let the last of her Scotch trickle down her throat. "What about alcohol or drugs? They can change a person, make them do things they normally wouldn't do."

"All the boys tested clean. Again, it was the next morning, and some or all of the effects could have worn off by then. I'll be honest with you, Rowan," Chloë said, looking at her. "Bryson does drink a little. I know he's underage, and we try to confine it to the home. We're trying to teach him that moderation is good, that alcohol can be part of the larger social milieu, and that getting plastered shouldn't be the end result."

"Hey, you won't get any criticism from me," Rowan replied. "You and I had to learn that the hard college way."

"We did let it rip a few times, didn't we?" Chloë agreed with a ghost of a smile.

"With varying results," Rowan said dryly. "I think we survived, though, and lived to enjoy another day. I'd love to take a wine-tasting course someday."

"If you have any questions, ask David. I'm honestly trying to get my head around everything in the wine cellar, but it's a slow process. On that note, would you like another Scotch?"

Rowan considered. "Sure, one more. Just another finger. I can get it."

"No, I'll do it. You're the guest." Chloë took Rowan's glass before she could protest.

Rowan folded her arms over the back of the sofa and rested her chin on them, watching Chloë at the bar. Her friend moved with a quick, precise, almost brittle rhythm, dropping ice cubes into the glass with silver tongs.

"I'm not sure if there's a polite way to ask this, but are you sure *you* should have another?" she asked.

An ice cube clattered on the sideboard and bounced onto the carpet.

Without turning, Chloë said, very quietly, "What do you mean?"

"I mean…in your condition."

Chloë finished fixing the drinks without speaking, although Rowan noticed that she'd changed her own selection to unadulterated sparkling water. Only after she came back around the sofa and gave Rowan her drink did she ask, "How long have you known?"

Not "how did you know?" Chloë was one of the few people who was privy to the knowledge of Rowan's ability.

"Since I hugged you at the station. I'm sorry, Chloë—I really didn't mean to pry. I was so tired that I let myself slip. The second I realized it, I shut it down."

Chloë took a deep breath. "It's okay, sweetie. I was planning on telling you, anyway. I'm barely three months along, and because of the miscarriage in May, I'm wary about announcing it too soon. David knows, of course, but we haven't told Bryson just yet. And now, with this other horrible mess…"

"I hope the stress won't cause problems with the baby," Rowan said, worried.

"So far, everything's okay," Chloë said. "I'm meditating every day, and drinking some herb tea that's supposed to help with relaxation. My doctor is wonderful for finding safe ways for me to deal with the stress, without resorting to drugs. Although he made it clear the occasional glass of wine is better than stress." She paused, biting her lip. "Could you… when you hugged me, could you tell if everything was okay?"

"I didn't sense anything wrong—although I wasn't looking for anything, and as soon as I realized you were pregnant, I backed off, because it was too personal. But no, nothing obvious leapt out at me. I could try again, if you'd like, but I don't know if I can actually suss out that sort of thing. Healing was Amanda's forte, not mine."

Chloë hesitated, and Rowan could tell she was trying to decide. Finally, Chloë said, "No, that's all right. If you didn't sense anything, then it's probably fine."

Rowan put her hand over Chloë's, sending some comforting energy and strength. Chloë closed her eyes, accepting the help. When they finished, she still looked wan, but re-invigorated.

"Thanks," Chloë said, smiling. "That felt good."

"I'm glad I could help."

Chloë's expression changed; now she looked intense again, and she gripped both of Rowan's hands. Her sculptor's fingers were long, supple, but cold and thin. "I'm not asking too much, am I? Asking you to help figure out what happened that night?"

"No, you're not." Rowan said, closing her eyes for a moment. "You wouldn't have asked me unless it was crucial. And I wouldn't be here if I didn't want to help."

"Thank you," Chloë whispered.

Rowan opened her eyes. "The thing is, I'm not entirely sure how I *can* help. I can't do anything that might interfere with the police investigation, and the only kid I'll definitely be able to talk to is Bryson—the other parents aren't going to appreciate some stranger bothering their kids."

"I've thought about it a bit," Chloë said. "First of all, the sheriff is a friend of the family's—hell, he's a friend of every family around here. He doesn't want to believe the boys did it, and although he's doing his job, I know he's going to be happier if it's proven that the boys didn't do it.

"The same goes for the other parents. I'm not sure if they'll all agree, but I'm pretty sure a couple of them will go along with it, if they think it might help prove their sons' innocence."

"I'm willing to do whatever I can, provided it's not breaking the law—too much," Rowan said.

Chloë smiled briefly. "Of course."

"Did you tell the sheriff about my ability?" Rowan asked.

"You said it would be okay, so I did."

"And?"

"He's skeptical. I'm sure he'll want to talk to you about it tomorrow."

Rowan sighed. "I can't say I'm looking forward to that, but if it'll help you and Bryson, it's worth it. Now, are you up to talking about the situation some more, or do you need a break?"

A burned-through log collapsed in the fireplace, sending a flurry of sparks up the chimney and the scent of burnt pine into the room.

Chloë shook her head. "Now that we're talking about it, I'd like to get it all out."

Rowan listened as her friend explained that the boys had been released on bail to the recognizance of their parents. The bail had been set at a moderate rate, she said, although Rowan realized it was actually quite high. High, at least, for those not of an upper-crust, upper-class background. David Waltham's family had invested in computers before computers were big, Rowan knew, but the money they'd invested had been old, family money. They'd already been well-off, and much the same was true of the other families in the community.

The four boys were confined to their homes unless accompanied by a parent or other adult authorized by the court. A tutor had been hired to continue their education so that they didn't fall behind in school, and all of them were regularly seeing a psychiatrist.

"That was part of the court arrangement, but we all would have insisted on it anyway," Chloë said. She picked up a baby pumpkin from the artistic autumn arrangement on the end table, and turned it over in her hands. "I just don't understand it, Rowan. If they didn't do it, why would they confess to it? Even the psychiatrist says their profiles don't fit that of a rapist or murderer. They're all completely torn up about this—shocked, upset."

"Repentant?" Rowan suggested.

"No." Chloë put the gourd down. "That's just it, Rowan. Like I said, they're absolutely horrified by it. But they don't seem remorseful. Oh, it's so hard to explain. Their reactions seem to be more like 'How could anybody do such a terrible thing?' rather than 'I did it, and I'm sorry.'"

"I don't know enough about psychology to comment on that one," Rowan said. "I'm sure the psychiatrist will make some headway there. Let's go back to the facts. So far, there's no physical evidence that puts them at the scene. What about witnesses? Did anyone see the crime? Do the boys have alibis for where they were supposed to be at the time?"

"Yes, that. Forensics placed the incident between 10:30 and 11:00 p.m. It was a school night, so all the boys should have been home or nearby. James was at Karl's, watching TV. Karl's father heard the TV on, but was in another part of the house and he can't swear they were home the whole time. Manny was at the gym swimming laps that evening, and the staff there said he left when the gym closed at 10:00. He said he then bicycled home as usual. No one remembers seeing him outside."

When Chloë didn't continue, Rowan prompted, "And Bryson?"

The gourd was in Chloë's hands again, turning over and over.

"David was away on a business trip that night," she said finally. "After dinner I went out to my studio—it's a converted guest house in the back—to work on some pieces for my show. Oh, I haven't told you about that. I will later. Anyway, I came down with a blinding headache all of a sudden, so I came back inside and decided to go to bed. Bryson was in his room, studying, I suppose. I called through the door that I was going to bed, and he commented that it was still early. I told him I wasn't feeling well, and he asked if there was anything he could do. I said no, and he said he hoped I felt better, and goodnight.

"There's a clock at the end of the hall, and I was looking straight as it while I was talking to Bryson. It was 10:45 p.m. There's no way he could have been gone and come back by that time, or that he could have left immediately afterwards and gotten to the woods in time.

"He was home, Rowan. I swear to you, he was home."

END OF PREVIEW

Waking the Witch is available in print or ebook from all your favorite retailers.

ABOUT THE AUTHOR

Dayle A. Dermatis is the author or coauthor of many novels (including snarky urban fantasy *Ghosted* and YA lesbian romance *Beautiful Beast*) and more than a hundred short stories in multiple genres, including fantasy and SF, romance, mystery, thriller, and YA.

Called the mastermind behind the Uncollected Anthology project, she also edits anthologies, and her own short fiction has been lauded in many year's best anthologies in erotica, mystery, and horror. Her romance fiction has been published in *Heart's Kiss* and various *Fiction River* anthologies, among others.

Dayle eloped properly in Gretna Green, Scotland, rode off on the back of a motorcycle, and hasn't looked back since except to smile and sigh happily. Unsurprisingly, she writes romances that are sometimes sweet, sometimes spicy, sometimes spooky, and sometimes funny, but will always make you smile and sigh happily.

An unabashed romantic, she lives in a historic English-style cottage with a wild and fae back garden, and whenever she can, she travels the world for inspiration and loses herself in music.

She'd love to have you over for a virtual cup of tea or glass of wine at DayleDermatis.com, where you can also sign up for her newsletter and support her on Patreon.

I value honest feedback, and would love to hear your opinion in a review, if you're so inclined, on your favorite book retailer's site.

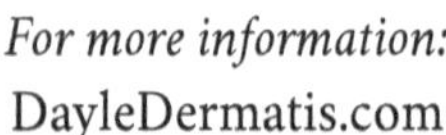

For more information:
DayleDermatis.com

BE THE FIRST TO KNOW!

Sign up for Dayle A. Dermatis's newsletter for *free* fiction, plus the latest news, releases, and more.

Sign up at DayleDermatis.com.

For more in-depth conversations and special sneak peeks, you can also support her continued work by joining her community of patrons out Dayle's Patreon.

Patreon.com/Dayle

www.ingramcontent.com/pod-product-compliance
Lightning Source LLC
Chambersburg PA
CBHW061808190726
48289CB00007B/2118